MW01228045

The Debt

An American Lawyer
Fights for Justice in Russia

Paul J. De Muniz

To Joann
With warm regards!
Paul

First published by Dog Ear Publishing
4011 Vincennes Rd
Indianapolis, IN 46268
www.dogearpublishing.net

ISBN: 978-1-4575-5103-1

This book is printed on acid-free paper.

Printed in the United States of America

To Vietnam war veterans.
Thank you for your service.

Acknowledgements

Thank you to the Russian judges, lawyers, and law professors, who taught me about their judicial system. A special thanks to my wonderful friends, Elena Wilson and Vadim Bourenin, from whom I learned so much about the Russian people. The time we shared in Russia created memories that will last my lifetime.

Author's Notes

Understanding Russian Names

Patronymic A Russian middle name is called a patronymic and is formed from the father's first name. A male's middle name is formed by the suffix *ovich* or *evich*. A female's middle name is formed by the suffix *ovna* or *evna*.

Surnames In general, Russian surnames are gender based. A female's surname is the same as a male's with an "a" added at the end.

Nicknames Russians commonly use affectionate nicknames—such as *Sasha* for Alexander and *Katya* for Yekaterina.

Russian Characters in the Book

Alexander Sergeevich Masterkov: senior investigator in the Sakhalin Island Regional Prokuror's (Attorney General's) office.

Olga Borisovna Sergova: investigative journalist for *Sovietsky Sakhalin*, the island's major newspaper.

Boris Stepanovich Sergov: Olga's father and Masterkov's mentor in Moscow.

Yekaterina "Katya" Osipova: Russian lawyer and co-counsel for Jonathan Haynes.

Yuri Karpov: Sakhalin Island Regional Prokuror (Attorney General for the region).

Natalia Kurilova: Olga Sergova's protégée at *Sovietsky Sakhalin*.

Mikhail Viktorovich Kurilov: Natalia Kurilova's father.

Boris Popov: government fingerprint expert.

Dr. Viktor Mitrokhin: veteran Sakhalin regional medical examiner.

Lyudmila Plotnikova: Masterkov's former lover.

Aleksey Pavlovich Vasilyuk: Chief Judge of the Sakhalin Regional Court.

Andrey Barbatov: deputy prokuror.

Ivan Dudinov: former Russian special forces officer and Sakhalin businessman.

Sergei Egorov: Russian army veteran.

Nadezhda: madam at Eurasia Hotel and Masterkov's cousin.

Tatiana Primakova: prostitute.

Prologue

Yuzhno-Sakhalinsk, Sakhalin Island, Russian Far East

The woman slept like a spent lover. She woke with hands around her neck. She screamed. Her arms and legs flailed. The man straddling her clamped his left hand over the woman's mouth. He drove his knee into her stomach and grabbed her neck. His hands felt cartilage tear and bones crack.

He lifted his hands, threw her ripped nightgown and panties to the floor, and pulled a penlight from his pocket. He cast the beam around the bedroom until the light rested on the woman's computer. He moved to the machine, pulled open a blade from a small imitation Swiss Army knife, and with great force peeled the hard drive from the interior of the computer. Using the penlight again, he located the woman's cell phone. He slipped the cell phone into his pocket and crept out of the apartment, descending the dark stairs of the apartment building and disappearing into the Russian night.

CHAPTER

1

Peter Chávez glanced at his right hand and saw the dried blood on the knuckle of his little finger. A thin red line ran down his white French cuff. He smiled, realizing he'd forgotten to remove his wedding ring before he'd smashed his right fist into his left hand during closing argument. This, he'd told the jury, was how forcefully the so-called victim had repeatedly punched his client. Suddenly, Chávez understood why some of the jurors seemed fixated on his hand. Not many lawyers, Chávez reflected, could actually claim that they had bled for their client.

Chávez focused on the jury-room door. In a moment a jury of seven women and five men would enter the courtroom, and Doug Stone would spend the rest of his life in prison or walk out of the courtroom a free man. Stone, a small-time drug dealer and thief, had offed his dipshit housemate over a meaningless marijuana sale. The case had attracted attention only because the housemate was a college football star before descending into criminality and drugs. Chávez had little interest in representing Stone, and he'd quoted Stone's mother a six-figure fee he thought she had no chance of paying. He was wrong.

In any event Chávez had long ago learned he didn't need to like his clients to defend them successfully. All he needed was the client's trust, and he had that. Stone and his mother had agreed to take the biggest gamble of all. They'd give the jury no middle ground, no lesser offenses like manslaughter that the jury could grasp as a compromise. The jury would make an all-or-nothing decision: self-defense or murder.

Tension pervaded the courtroom, but Chávez appeared unflappable, just as courtroom regulars expected. Only a couple of the city's retired lawyers, old-timers sitting in the back of the courtroom, knew how unlikely it was that Chávez would be standing where he stood now. He seldom thought of those days, at least not in the grand old courtroom where, over the years, he had grown so comfortable and now waited for the verdict. Chávez had graduated from law school with excellent grades and even made law review. Today every large firm wanted at least one lawyer with an easily-identifiable Hispanic surname, but in those days most of the big Portland firms had ignored him. Or maybe his ethnicity wasn't the problem. His working-class roots worked against him too. He was different from the young lawyers sent to recruit his law school's graduates. Chávez assumed the interviewers could tell that he did not want to be like them, and they apparently wanted to hire lawyers just like themselves. They were privileged. He was not. Most of them had found a way to avoid serving in Vietnam. Chávez had volunteered.

For Bill Wright, a sole practitioner in Oregon's state capital, Chávez's ethnicity and the modest circumstances of his upbringing were irrelevant. Wright wanted a young, smart, and aggressive lawyer to help with his burgeoning criminal practice. In only a year Chávez was making a name for himself and attracting his own clients. Word traveled fast in the criminal milieu. Chávez spoke three languages—English, Spanish, and Russian. The Spanish he'd mastered in college, not at home as most people assumed. The Russian he'd learned thanks to the U.S. Army and its Monterey Language Institute, though the Army never got the full value for what they'd spent on that training. But Wright would. Around Salem, Mexican farm hands and young men from a local Russian Old Believers settlement often ended up ensnared in the county's criminal-justice system, fairly accused or not.

Still, in the early days Chávez experienced subtle and sometimes not-so-subtle questions about his ethnicity. Some judges seemed reluctant to appoint him to more serious cases, even though he had demonstrated from the beginning that he was good in the courtroom— really good. One of those reluctant judges, now the most senior judge in the state, was presiding over the current trial. Judge Val Parks, a white haired, jowly man, had come around, and now he revered Chávez's courtroom savvy.

But this case was different. Inside, Chávez felt unaccustomed tension. Stone's trial could well be Chávez's last as a criminal defense lawyer.

He turned and glanced at the two retired lawyers in the back of the courtroom. One of them looked around the courtroom and flashed a thumbs-up. Chávez winked and turned back to the jury-room door, projecting confidence he did not feel.

Stone flinched as the jury-room door sprang open. Helen Clarke, juror number eleven, clutched the folded verdict in her hand. Chávez's heart rate normalized. Chávez had kept her on the jury despite the fact that she was married to a successful businessman in Salem, well-known as a right-wing nut who was a hardliner on criminal justice. But Helen Clarke, in her mid-forties, had struck Chávez as a woman who was independent-minded and admired competence—something the prosecutor clearly lacked. After questioning Clarke, Chávez had been confident of one thing. If he left Clarke on the jury, she would emerge as the foreperson. And that would augur well for his case.

Doug Stone and Jerry Hall had shared a trashy house they used to retail dope and stolen motorcycle parts. It was Hall, the former college linebacker, who pummeled the smaller Stone over Stone's failure to share the proceeds of a marijuana deal. Before he collapsed, Stone managed to pull a Ruger pistol from his back pocket and fire. The bullet entered Hall's brain through his left eye socket, killing him instantly.

Those facts made for a good self-defense case. But Stone had admitted to the police that he'd armed himself with the Ruger intending to use it against Hall in the confrontation that he knew was coming. Chávez, however, believed that he'd found the evidence to counter that problem.

Two of the jurors had wept as they listened to the testimony of Dr. Jeff Rogers, Hall's doctor and a member of Oregon's mountain rescue team. Chávez was surprised that a lowlife like Hall even had a doctor and even more surprised at what Rogers revealed in a routine pre-trial interview. In court, Chávez had Rogers describe in vivid detail how Hall had threatened to kill him and his family unless he agreed to Hall's repeated requests for narcotics. Rogers' testimony put the victim on trial. Jurors could legitimize their feelings that the world was a better place without Jerry Hall in it.

As the last juror took his seat, Judge Parks looked up from his magazine and asked for the verdict form. Clarke rose and presented the folded paper to the bailiff. The bailiff handed the verdict form to Parks who studied it without giving a hint of the decision. As Judge Parks studied the verdict form, Clarke looked directly at Chávez. Chávez thought that her eyes communicated respect for a job well done. Judge Parks finished reading the verdict form and slowly raised his eyes over the rim of his reading glasses. For an instant Parks looked directly at Stone. The mounting sense of euphoria inside Chávez suddenly subsided, replaced by dread. In a deep authoritative voice Judge Parks told Stone to stand for the reading of the verdict. As was his custom, Chávez rose beside his client. Parks wasted no time with preliminaries. Hardly glancing at the verdict form, Parks quoted, "We the jury find the above-named defendant, Douglas Stone, not guilty of the crime of murder."

As Parks read the word "not," Evelyn Stone leaned across the railing toward her son. Deputies in the courtroom started to move forward, but then froze, allowing mother and son to embrace. Angry noises came from the courtroom area that Hall's family and friends had occupied during the trial. Judge Parks did not bang the gavel for order. Instead, he pretended to study some paperwork in front of him and waited for the commotion to die down naturally. Hall's family and friends left the courtroom, glaring at the jury as they did. Chávez shook hands with mother and son, opened his trial notebook, and wrote, "Not Guilty, 4:30 p.m., December 20, 2005."

Chávez made eye contact with each juror as they filed from the jury box. Clarke nodded as she departed. Chávez permitted himself a return smile. One last item remained. After all of the jurors had left the courtroom, Judge Parks asked Evelyn Stone to return to her seat on the other side of the railing. Parks then told Doug Stone that he was free to go. A look passed between Chávez and Judge Parks. Stone was free to go all right, back to his mostly crappy existence—but how long would it be before Stone would do something else that was criminally stupid?

Television and newspaper reporters crowded Chávez, Stone, and his mother as they emerged from the courtroom. An attractive woman from a Portland TV station was the first to shove a microphone in Chávez's face. Other reporters pushed Stone and his mother aside.
"Were you confident from the beginning that the jury would acquit your client? Is this your last case?"

Chávez did not answer immediately. Instead, he paused to sort through his thoughts, getting them in the right order. He started with his standard response to the first question.

"Yes, I was confident that when all the evidence was put before the jury, they would do the right thing."

The second question—the last he would answer—involved a flood of emotions. Chávez was one of Oregon's most successful criminal defense lawyers and the state's most visible Latino lawyer. If things went right, his identity as a trial lawyer would end. Now, just shy of 60, he was about to realize what he wanted most in his legal career. "Yes, this is my last case as a trial lawyer. Law practice has been good to me. However, I am looking forward to a new challenge."

There were other questions about the case. Chávez answered those questions patiently and thoroughly. He ignored the additional questions about his pending career change. Chávez glanced at his watch. It was six o'clock, and the courthouse was nearly empty. He was tempted to walk to the watering hole directly across the street from the courthouse for a couple of drinks with some of the local lawyers and judges. The two retired lawyers who had followed the trial were sure to be there. Having a drink or two and receiving the congratulations from good friends might help him avoid the emptiness and uncertainty that now plagued him in his solitary moments.

Chávez paused at the bottom of the courthouse steps, then turned left toward the courthouse parking lot. He had an early morning flight to Washington, D.C.

* * * * * * * * *

Chávez had begun the process of applying for a vacant position on the federal bench in Portland more than a year earlier. After a series of interviews with a statewide judicial screening committee, the committee had selected Chávez and two other lawyers as the most qualified candidates and had forwarded their names to Oregon's two senators. Despite the committee's enthusiastic recommendation, Chávez had anticipated that Oregon's senior Republican senator, John Garlock, whose turn it was to submit a candidate's name to the president, would be a problem. Garlock, the heir to one of Oregon's largest timber fortunes, was an arch-conservative—all about law and order. However, after two personal meetings, Garlock expressed his enthusiastic support and forwarded Chávez's name to the president. The president had followed Garlock's recommendation and had nominated Chávez two months before the start of the Stone trial.

This third meeting in Garlock's Washington, D.C. Senate office was at Garlock's request. Garlock's staff had not disclosed the specifics of the meeting. Chávez had been sitting in the waiting room for a few minutes when the senator, a large man over six foot five attired in a perfectly-fitted Armani suit, invited Chávez inside the spacious and beautifully decorated office in the Russell Building.

Although Chávez had been inside the senator's office for two previous meetings, he was again awestruck by the photos of America's most famous people. The photos of various sizes covered nearly every inch of every wall. As best as Chávez could observe every photo was signed by the subject or subjects. For just a moment Chávez let his eyes return to his favorite—the signed photo of Babe Ruth that he had discovered during his first visit to the senator's office. "Good to see you, Pete," Garlock began the conversation, stretching his long legs out in front of him.

"Also a pleasure, Senator," Chávez replied. "I am grateful for your support."

"That is why I wanted you here. Let's talk about where we are in this deal."

Although Garlock's tone sounded casual, Chávez could sense that the senator had something specific on his mind.

"Of course, Senator. Is there something more I need to do?"

"No. It's more about what you *shouldn't* do."

Chávez's heart pounded, anticipating which conservative group was now against his nomination.

"You know," said Garlock, "I'm no fan of criminal defense lawyers. Hell, my support for you caused a lot of folks to wet their pants. But you're a straight-shooter, and the Oregon cops like you. And I don't figure you'll be any goddamned Earl Warren. You'll follow the law, right? And the low-life perps won't get any valentines from your court. Right?"

Garlock paused, and Chávez broke in, "Yessir. I believe in the law."

"You betcha. But I'm not your problem, Chávez. The president went along with me and nominated you. But he's got his nightie in a knot over this. The evangelicals aren't completely pissed about your nomination, but they're starting to make noises. Two Republican senators on the judiciary committee have already bitched to me about you representing crackheads and perverts. And they're especially wired about the two death penalty cases you got overturned by the Nine."

Chávez kept a poker face. He was proud of those Supreme Court cases and had allowed himself to believe that he was past the whole criminal defense thing. Oregon's Attorney General and the Oregon District Attorney's Association were among his strongest supporters.

"I understand, Senator. You know that I'm Catholic. So what are these guys complaining about? It's still about those death penalty cases, isn't it? What can I do to put the lid on that one?"

"Well, now there seems to be a bit more," the senator replied. "Apparently, you had a case in which you got a burglar who shot and killed the homeowner acquitted of aggravated murder. I mean not only did the guy escape the death penalty, you got the jury to find him not guilty of murder in what I understand was an open-and-shut case for the prosecution. I guess the guy did something like three years for burglary, but that's all. Oh, and somehow you convinced a judge to let you back into the victim's house so you could do your own forensic tests. There are newspaper stories someone dug up on the internet that are circulating among the evangelicals recounting the widow pleading with the judge not to let you in her house. As she said, 'so you could prove her husband was a drunk and get your guy off.'"

As the senator paused, Chávez cut in. "Senator, there is a lot more to that case than you have been told. The alleged victim tried to execute the defendant. It was complicated, but the result was correct. That was ten years ago." Senator Garlock held up his hand. "Relax, that's why I asked you to come back to Washington. I have arranged for you to visit this afternoon with those two colleagues of mine, and one of the evangelical leaders. I am sure you have heard of Ned Richter, he runs the Coalition for Christian and Family Values. I believe that once Richter meets you personally, as I did, all of this will go away. He also admires Vietnam veterans. Be sure to let him know that you served in Vietnam. Of course, the official senatorial visits will occur the week before the Senate Judiciary Committee hearings. You should be in town by March 20th. That will give us a full week before the hearing on the 27th."

Chávez had seen Ned Richter on TV. Richter was one of those super patriots who had never worn the uniform. He seemed to be what Chávez's grandfather would have described as a "sanctimonious, psalm-singing son of a bitch." Chávez was sure he could say the right things to the two senators. However, with Richter it would take every ounce of self-control.

"Thank you for arranging these meetings in advance. I am deeply grateful," Chávez replied, keeping to himself what he was tempted to say to Richter.

"No problem. Let's go talk to those guys," Garlock announced, adding, "I assume you are winding down your practice. I heard that you won that Stone case in Salem. I don't think anyone cared about that since the guy Stone shot was such a dirtbag. I am sure I don't need to tell you, however, anything controversial between now and the hearings could put your nomination in jeopardy."

CHAPTER

2

Alexander Sergeevich Masterkov lifted the crime scene tape and stepped through the front door of the spartanly-furnished flat in the eastern reaches of the city of Yuzhno-Sakhalinsk. Just inside the door uniformed *militsiya* directed Masterkov to the bedroom.

As he walked through the small flat, Masterkov removed his black sable hat and three-quarter-length fur trimmed overcoat, revealing his blue military-style uniform. As he did, he noticed an unfamiliar young woman in a *militsiya* uniform staring at him. He smiled at her, and she quickly turned away. It had been going on since high school. With his hat and overcoat on, he appeared typically Russian. However, his appearance changed dramatically when those outer garments were removed. His hair was a striking auburn color and thick. His face was almond shaped, with a light sprinkling of reddish freckles. It was the unique combination that defied the typical Russian categories—Nordic, Cossack, eastern Asiatic. He assumed the young woman concluded that at fifty he was still good-looking, though not in the usual Russian way.

As the senior investigator in the Sakhalin Island Regional Prokuror's Office, it was his job to supervise the crime scene and manage what undoubtedly would be a homicide investigation. Masterkov had seen hundreds of corpses. He assumed this was another routine homicide likely fueled by too much vodka. The killer was probably in custody or would be soon.

Masterkov's countenance faded as he entered the bedroom and came into full view of the body. Instantly, he averted his eyes, fighting to suppress the bile forcing its way up his throat. When he raised his eyes there was no doubt. The naked body sprawled on the bed was Olga Sergova, the daughter of Boris Stepanovich Sergov, Masterkov's criminal law professor at Moscow State University and the man who had mentored him during his early years with a special *militsiya* homicide unit in Moscow. In that position Masterkov had gotten sideways with some powerful people in Moscow. It was Sergov who saved Masterkov and his career by engineering a transfer to the Russian Far East. Professor Sergov had died only a year earlier, worried but proud of his only daughter, an investigative journalist for *Sovietsky Sakhalin*, the island's major newspaper.

There was more, however. Soon after Olga had arrived on the island she had contacted him. Immediately, they began secretly sharing information back and forth. She had helped him secure evidence in two major corruption cases. They always met in some out-of-the-way place. Although he knew that Olga lived in this area of the city, he had never been to her apartment.

A few days earlier she had left a message on his cell phone. Olga thought that she was on to something very big. She wanted him to know about it. They were going to meet after Christmas.

Having suppressed the immediate involuntary reaction he first felt in seeing Olga's body, Masterkov began another involuntary thought process. Long ingrained from Soviet times, Masterkov focused on how he should react outwardly to the death of the daughter of a man he had loved almost like a father. Masterkov was sure that none of the *militsiya* in the apartment, his boss Yuri Karpov, the region's Prokuror General, nor anyone on the island for that matter, knew about his relationship with Professor Boris Sergov or Sergov's daughter. Masterkov concluded that who better than he, someone with a personal interest, to investigate Olga's murder. And there was no other investigator in the prosecutor's office that he truly trusted.

Masterkov pulled a new pair of rubber gloves from his right coat pocket. Outwardly, it was business as usual. His eyes scanned the room completely then focused on a pair of panties lying next to the bed, nearly ripped in half, likely torn from Olga's beautiful body. Methodically, Masterkov moved his eyes around the area by the bed. There was a nightshirt on the floor next to the bed. Most of the buttons were missing and scattered on the floor. On a chair near the bed he observed a pair of women's Levi's and a black turtleneck sweater. Curiously, both items were folded neatly. A bra was on top of the Levi's and sweater.

He leaned over the body, beginning his examination for pre- and post-mortem injuries. Olga's black hair was long and thick, had a shiny quality to it, and gave off a pleasing citrus smell. Masterkov felt his face flush as an inner battle erupted. Feelings of self-loathing invaded what was supposed to be a methodical forensic examination. He could not help himself—she was stunning. She had been a rower at the University in St. Petersburg, nearly Olympic caliber. She had obviously worked to maintain her trim athletic figure. Masterkov had been strongly attracted to her the moment of their first meeting. He had thought about her a lot that way but had concluded that their nearly twenty-year age difference was too much. In any event she had always kept things professional.

Olga's eyes, frozen open in death, were blue like her father's. Masterkov bent to within inches of her head, peering into her eyes. As he suspected, the pinhead-sized petechial hemorrhages, common to strangulation victims, were present.

Automatically Masterkov's eyes moved to her neck. There were faint reddish marks on the skin. She had been strangled, either by hand or with some type of ligature. The body was cold to his touch. He moved her right arm; the stiffness indicated that rigor was present. He could not tell with any precision, however, how long she had been dead.

His eyes moved down her torso, stopping at her perfectly flat stomach. A large, undifferentiated red bruise was present just above her belly button. Something hard had struck her squarely in the stomach. He could not identify any signs of trauma or bruising to the visible parts of her genitalia. Her lean, long legs also were unmarred.

Masterkov turned from the body and again glanced about the room. It was small, typical of the bedrooms of the Khrushchev-era apartments that dominated the cities of the Russian Far East. In addition to the bed, which was unmade and in disarray, there was an end table and a dresser. In one corner there were a couple of pairs of running shoes and some running shorts and shirts. A laptop computer, its hard drive apparently ripped out, was on the floor near a small desk. All the drawers of the desk and the nearby dresser were open or overturned on the carpeted floor. Women's clothes were scattered about the floor.

Masterkov sensed the criminalists from the forensics laboratory enter the bedroom preparing to commence an inch-by-inch inspection of the apartment looking for evidence that might provide clues to the identity of the killer. Masterkov made eye contact with the supervisor and signaled his permission for them to begin. For just a minute Masterkov looked up and watched them begin to unpack the tools and implements they would use in an attempt to gather evidence from the apartment. They unloaded a small vacuum, which they would use to suction up loose hairs, fibers and other trace evidence that might be found on the body and in the apartment. Later, when Masterkov prepared and forwarded his questions to the region's medical examiner, he would direct the medical examiner to collect any hair, fiber, skin and fluid evidence found in or on Olga's body during the autopsy.

One of the criminalists approached Masterkov and informed him that a fingerprint expert was on the way to the apartment and inquired whether Masterkov had touched anything. His face impassive, Masterkov raised both hands showing the rubber gloves and said, "No, except that I touched her right arm to determine if rigor was present." Masterkov then left the bedroom and approached the *militsiya* supervisor in the living room. Outwardly, he was following protocol.

"What do we know at this point?"

The supervisor nodded, flipped open his small spiral notebook, and matter-of-factly replied, "The victim is Olga Borisovna Sergova, a newspaper reporter. I am sure you have heard of her. She's that investigative reporter always putting her nose where it's not wanted. She won't be doing that anymore. Obviously, she had any number of enemies."

Masterkov nodded slightly, concealing his desire to slap away the supervisor's shitty grin.

"She lived alone. Her friend, Natalia Michelevna Kurilova, discovered the body about an hour ago. She is downstairs in a patrol car."

Masterkov instructed the supervisor to begin interviewing the other apartment residents. He then retrieved his coat and hat. On the way out he examined the apartment door. There was the usual dead bolt and handle lock. Neither lock appeared to be forced. Both could be manipulated easily with the right tools. He was surprised that Olga apparently had not thought it necessary to have better security.

Masterkov walked down the three flights of stairs to the ground level, opened the outer door of the building to a blast of arctic air, and looked over to the patrol car. Through the frosted windows of the compact patrol car, Masterkov could see that a young blonde woman was huddled in one corner of the back seat. A veteran *militsiya* officer sat in the front. The car was running, presumably, to provide some heat for the woman in the backseat. She had her head in her hands. Her whole body shook.

Olga had mentioned Natalia Kurilova on a couple of occasions. According to Olga, Kurilova was bright and completely loyal to Olga. He doubted, however, that Kurilova knew about the secret relationship he had with Olga. Masterkov walked briskly to the patrol car, opened the driver's side rear door, dismissed the officer in the front seat, and introduced himself as he slid onto the seat next to her. The woman lowered her hands from her head and looked at him from under a brown cheaply-made beaver fur hat. Masterkov did not see any glimmer of recognition in her eyes.

He began in a soft voice. "I understand that you are acquainted with Olga Sergova. I would like to know when you last saw her alive."

Kurilova gathered herself and responded, "Oh, we work together, you know, at *Sovietsky Sakhalin*. She is a reporter. I do research and administrative things for her and other reporters. I liked Olga. We were good friends."

How good? Masterkov wondered, now not as completely confident that she did not know about his relationship with Olga. He said nothing, his face impassive, waiting for Kurilova to continue.

"Olga and I had agreed to meet for tea this morning to discuss something she was working on. There were things she wanted me to run down. She did not show up and was not in the office when I arrived. It was not like Olga not to at least call me. When she still had not come in or called by eleven a.m., I decided to call her. I tried to call her cell phone three times in an hour. It was weird. The phone would ring and ring and then go to some kind of standard voice mail."

Silently Masterkov recorded the peculiar information about the cell phone in his memory bank. He had not observed a cell phone in the apartment or among the items that appeared to have been dumped from Olga's purse. Olga's number was preserved in his personal cell phone. He would try calling her number in a few minutes. Kurilova halted, so Masterkov asked, "Why did you come here?"

Kurilova's voice rose an octave as she continued.

"It was just so unlike Olga that I decided to come over here. Perhaps she was sick or something and could not call or answer the phone."

Masterkov nodded and asked, "What time did you arrive?"

Kurilova appeared to think for a moment. Then she said, "I had to take a bus, so it took me about thirty minutes. I got here a little before one o'clock."

Kurilova sobbed, and in a halting voice she said, "I knocked on her door, and I said, 'Olga, Olga.' I turned the handle on the door, and it opened. I called her name again, and she did not answer. I don't know why, I just ran into her bedroom."

Masterkov asked, "What about the dead bolt lock?"

Ignoring the question, Kurilova began to wail, "She was murdered, someone murdered her—they got her."

Masterkov let Kurilova compose herself and then asked, "Who are 'they?' Do you know who killed her?"

Kurilova, still with her head in her hands, replied in a helpless voice, "I don't know, we work on stories that some people don't like, powerful people, who knows."

Masterkov could sense that she was pulling back, thinking she had already said too much to someone in the government. He assumed that Kurilova was like the average Russian; she likely thought that the police were corrupt and that Masterkov might alert the killer or killers that she knew something important and would be the next victim.

He pressed forward.

"What were you working on now? Was that what you were going to meet about this morning?"

Kurilova hesitated. Masterkov again assumed that she was calculating whether to answer truthfully, "Nothing specific, looking at some things about the oil and gas companies. I am really not sure," she said looking away from him.

There it was—the oil and gas companies. Masterkov would have to listen again to Olga's last message on his cell phone. She had mentioned the oil and gas companies; however, she also said that her investigation could lead to people in the highest government positions. Masterkov was sure Kurilova knew more, but he doubted it would be forthcoming. He continued, "Have there been any threats?"

Kurilova looked at the floor of the patrol car and said, "No, not that Olga ever told me about, but you know how it is."

He knew how it was; investigative journalism was a dangerous occupation in Russia. Over the past few years, fourteen reporters had been killed in Russia, three killed in the Russian Far East. The editor of *Forbes Russia*, Paul Klebnikov, an American, had been murdered outside his office in Moscow. It was assumed that all of the previous murders of journalists were contract hits. They were assumed because not a single one of those cases had been prosecuted. Olga Sergova's murder would make a total of fifteen. The others were different, however. They had all been shot or car bombed. Contract killers seemed not to be the strangling type.

Kurilova crossed her arms on her chest, as if to say I am done talking. He would talk to Kurilova again. Hopefully, the next time she would reveal the nature of Sergova's investigation into the oil and gas companies' affairs. There was, however, one more question. "I know that Sergova was not married, but did she have a relationship, or was she dating someone?"

Kurilova again paused, and with little affect stated, "What do you think? Olga was beautiful. She dated men from time to time, but I don't think she was dating anyone regularly right now, at least not that I know of."

Masterkov was not sure what the last part of her answer meant. Was she implying that Olga had a secret lover? Again he showed no outward interest in the comment.

Instead, he said, "I will need a list of the men Ms. Sergova dated. Under Russian law, you may not speak to anyone else about this. You may speak only to me or another investigator from my office. I suggest for your own safety that you do not speak to anyone else about this. I will have the *militsiya* drive you to your apartment." Kurilova nodded but gave no verbal response.

"Oh, before you go. What kind of computer did Ms. Sergova use? Did she use more than one computer, perhaps one at work?" Masterkov added, picturing the laptop on the bedroom floor, the hard drive gone.

"She used only her laptop. She took it with her almost everywhere she went," Kurilova replied.

"Thank you. I am sorry about your friend."

Kurilova did not reply.

Masterkov watched the small patrol car with Kurilova huddled in the back maneuver away from the apartment building around and over the ruts carved in the ice and frozen mud toward the snow-covered road. The billions of dollars invested in the multinational oil and gas projects were supposed to bring prosperity to the residents of Sakhalin Island, the poorest region in Russia. Little had trickled down to local residents. It was the oil and gas projects that had brought Olga to Sakhalin, away from Russia's great cities of St. Petersburg and Moscow. She had assumed that the billions of dollars connected to the oil and gas projects would breed corruption at the highest levels. Of course, she was right. Was Olga now a victim of the violence and corruption that had accompanied the new Russia's commitment to a free-market society, or was she just a random murder victim?

A deep sadness swept over Masterkov as he watched the car disappear. He had loved Olga's father as if he were his own. Somehow Boris Sergov had succeeded in the KGB and later as a law professor without ever overtly compromising his integrity. Masterkov had long ago given up trying to measure up to that standard. However, Professor Sergov would want Masterkov to work on the case personally and to take the investigation wherever it led—no matter where.

The investigation of the murder of Olga Sergova would be different from the investigations of the murders of the all other Russian journalists. This murder would be competently investigated and solved, Masterkov almost said aloud as he trudged back up the apartment building's stairs to complete his supervision of the crime scene examination.

* * * * * * * * * *

Masterkov munched on leftover *perozki* as he read the autopsy report submitted by Dr. Viktor Mitrokhin, the veteran Sakhalin regional medical examiner. The report answered each of the questions that Masterkov had directed to the medical examiner following Masterkov's observations of Olga's body and examination of Olga's apartment. As Masterkov expected, Mitrokhin's autopsy determined that Olga Sergova had been strangled. Mitrokhin noted the petechial hemorrhages present in the eyes and the reddish marks on the neck that Masterkov had observed when he first examined the body at the crime scene. In addition, Mitrokhin recorded that the hyoid bone was broken, which was further confirmation that Olga had been strangled. The broken hyoid bone was also some measure of the lethality of the pressure that had been applied to Olga's neck. There was a large bruise present on Olga's abdomen that Mitrokhin concluded was likely sustained in the struggle preceding her death. Mitrokhin noted that by the time he had examined the body, rigor was no longer present. Based on his lab analysis of the digestive state of Olga's stomach contents and of the potassium level in the vitreous fluid of her eyes, Mitrokhin estimated that Olga had been killed twelve to twenty-four hours before Kurilova had discovered her body, probably on the evening of December 20th or the early morning hours of the 21st.

In response to one of Masterkov's routine questions Mitrokhin also reported that, according to established autopsy protocol, he had swabbed Olga's mouth and vagina to collect fluid samples. Nothing of evidentiary significance was noted from the lab analysis of the fluid from her mouth. However, examination of the fluid from her vagina revealed seminal fluid and motile sperm. Masterkov knew that sperm could remain motile for a number of hours after discharge.

Mitrokhin's report described areas of irritation and reddening in the vagina, asserting that the irritation and reddening that he observed was consistent with sexual assault. Masterkov was not so sure. In his experience trauma to the vagina was usually much greater in cases of sexual assault than Mitrokhin's observations revealed.

A black pubic hair, which Mitrokhin determined was foreign, had been found mingled with Olga's pubic

hair. Human skin material was found under the finger-
nail of Olga's right index finger. Masterkov was confident
that the semen, sperm, hair and skin material could eventually be used as DNA sources to confirm the identity of
a killer-rapist.

Masterkov looked away from the report to think for
a moment. Whether or not Mitrokhin was correct in
asserting that Olga had been raped, one thing was certain. The semen and the irritation and reddening in the
vagina meant she was penetrated before she was strangled. Contract killers, however, shot their victims or blew
them up in their cars. Contract killers did not rape and
strangle their victims.

Masterkov's vibrating cell phone jolted him from
his thoughts.

"Alexander Sergeevich, its Boris Popov."

"Yes," Masterkov responded.

"I need to see you as soon as possible."

"What is it? Do you have a fingerprint?" Masterkov
inquired eagerly.

Popov ignored the question. "How soon can you get
over to the lab?"

"I am on my way," Masterkov replied, pressing the
end button on his cell phone.

It was windy with lightly-falling snow blowing on
top of the dirty snow covering the streets. Masterkov
barely noticed the flakes blowing directly at him, as he
tramped the two blocks to Popov's lab, lost in thoughts
about what he had just read in Mitrokhin's autopsy
report and why Popov had called him over to the lab
instead of emailing his report as was the usual protocol.

Masterkov found Popov in the fingerprint section of the crime lab. He was staring fixedly at a computer with two digital fingerprints on the screen, side by side.

Masterkov cleared his throat, "Boris, I am here. What is so urgent? Do you have a print match in the Sergova case?"

Popov turned his round chalk-colored face from the computer screen, swiveling in his chair slightly and motioning for Masterkov to pull up a nearby chair. Popov began before Masterkov could say a word.

"As you directed I dusted and used the new laser technique throughout Sergova's apartment. A number of latent prints were found at the scene. I determined that there were ten usable prints and looked for a match in the Integrated Automated Fingerprint Identification System."

Masterkov nodded but said nothing. Popov had explained the laser technique and how the IAFIS worked at least ten times. Masterkov remained skeptical of the accuracy of digital imagery. He had once seen a comparison of a digital picture of a map containing the word Moscow compared to a 35mm picture of the same portion of the map. On the digital image the word Moscow was missing the "s."

Popov continued, providing Masterkov with details about the fingerprint identification system that he already knew. "There are forty-five million print records in IAFIS. IAFIS returned possible matches on eight of the ten prints. Three of the prints were Sergova's. A right thumb and right index finger were identified as Kurilova's, ah, the woman who found her. They found those on the inside door handle of the apartment's entry door. Two others were from *militsiya* personnel who were at the scene. The right thumbprint of Rukavets, the *militsiya* supervisor, was found on the outer door handle, and the left index fingerprint of Falaleev, one of the first *militsiya* to enter the apartment, was found on the interior side of the door. There were two on the laptop that could not be matched."

Afraid that Popov would somehow talk for an hour without getting to the point, Masterkov broke in, "Okay, that is seven that you matched. You said there were eight matches."

Popov nodded.

"Well," Masterkov said, trying to suppress his frustration, "What about the other match?"

"Well, yes, let me explain number eight fully. Print number eight was found on one of two wine glasses on the drain board in the kitchen. Sergova's right index finger, right ring finger, and right thumb were found on one of the glasses. Number eight was on the other wine glass. The print is a right index finger and it's perfectly preserved."

"Perfectly preserved." The words rang like a chime in Masterkov's head. Sure it is, Masterkov thought. But this was Russia. Something will surely go wrong before we can use this print.

Popov swiveled back to the computer, motioning for Masterkov to lean in close.

"The print on the right side of the screen is the number eight print lifted from the wine glass in Sergova's apartment. The print on the left side of the screen is a digital copy from IAFIS."

Popov paused, and then as if he had just scored the winning goal in a hockey game, he got up from his chair and put his right arm in the air.

"Alexander, there is no question here. I have over fifteen points of identification. I have even done a level-three comparison that matches ridge edges, ridge marks, and the pores. It's a one hundred-percent match. Alexander, we know who left that print."

CHAPTER

3

Chávez opened the garage door, unaware that it had snowed during the evening, distracted by images and thoughts of Claire and the crappy Christmas that he had spent alone. The stroke had happened quickly. An undetected brain aneurysm had burst. Claire died in the ambulance on the way to the hospital. There were no children; he was completely alone. Every morning for the past three years he had started the day hoping his mood would brighten, that the dull ache that periodically gripped his body would simply disappear. Assuming the Senate confirmed his nomination, he hoped that his new life on the federal bench, free of the pressures of law practice—pressures he loved and sometimes hated at the same time—might change things.

There was only about an inch of snow on the ground, but the streets were covered. Morning traffic, even on a Saturday in a small city like Salem, would be snarled. People in the Northwest were not accustomed to snow, so even a small amount caused chaos. He decided to walk to the office. The dry snow squeaked under his feet as Chávez made his way toward Lee

House, the historic home that he and Claire had converted to a law office.

He had been in the office for about an hour when the phone rang, rousing Chávez from his thoughts about his new life without clients. Although surprised that the office phone would ring on a Saturday, Chávez instinctively punched the button and picked up the receiver. A weak raspy voice said, "This is Michael Haynes. Is this Peter?"

"Who did you say this is?" Chávez responded loudly into the phone.

This time the voice on the other end answered in a low but firm voice, "Peter, this is Michael Haynes from Vietnam."

Chávez simply said, "Okay," involuntarily glancing at the raised red shrapnel scar on the top of his left wrist—his only remaining visible scar. The voice started again, "I know it has been a long time. But please listen to me."

"Yes, it sure has," was all that Chávez could manage in response. His mind, however, was operating at warp speed, at once trying to calculate why Haynes was calling him and also reliving the event that had forever joined them together. The VC rocket attack had caught Chávez in the open. The first rocket had hit just close enough to throw Chávez's body into the air like a rag doll as he was speared with metal shards. Chávez lay in the open, unable to raise himself, as everything around him exploded. Suddenly, large hands had gripped Chávez's torso and pulled him agonizingly, foot by foot, to a makeshift bunker. One second more above the ground, and there would have been nothing left to send home in a body bag.

Michael Haynes, the man who had saved Chávez, had returned to the states by the time Chávez was released from the Qui Nhon Hospital to return to his unit. Two years after returning from Vietnam, Chávez located Haynes in Seattle, where Haynes claimed to be attending the University of Washington. To Chávez's surprise, Haynes lived in an expensive apartment in the Madison Park district of Seattle and drove a new Corvette. Haynes was big, about six foot four, and athletically built. He had a smile that spread across his face from ear to ear. Although Chávez liked Haynes instantly, he easily concluded that Haynes' Corvette and expensive apartment were not the result of a rich family—rich boys did not serve as combat soldiers in Vietnam. Although the meeting was cordial and Haynes graciously accepted Chávez's thanks for saving his life, he revealed little about himself or his future plans during their time together in Seattle. After the meeting with Haynes, as he drove home, Chávez reasoned that his savior in Vietnam was likely a high-level drug dealer. Whether Haynes began his lucrative business in the Central Highlands of Vietnam had struck Chávez as an interesting question.

Chávez held the phone to his ear waiting for Haynes' next words. He assumed that the conclusion he had drawn about Haynes more than thirty years earlier was about to be confirmed. Haynes probably was now charged in some drug conspiracy in federal court in Portland.

"Peter, my son, Jonathan, is in trouble. He's charged with murder. I need your help." Haynes stated in precise measured phrases. Gone was the jive talk and slang that had been a part of their earlier meeting.

Chávez cleared his throat. "Of course. Is he here in Oregon? Are you still in Seattle? Is he in Seattle? I know some excellent lawyers there. Don't worry, I can get him a lawyer wherever he is."

Again the voice in response was weak, as if the person was struggling for air. "Yes, I am still in Seattle. No, my son Jonathan is not in Seattle. He's not in the United States. He's in Russia, the Russian Far East. Jonathan is a petroleum engineer for ExxonMobil. He works on the island of Sakhalin, just north of Japan. Have you heard of that place?"

Chávez thought for a moment. Sakhalin Island. Then he remembered, "Isn't that somewhere near the place where the Soviets shot down a Korean airliner with some Americans on board the plane?"

"Yes, that's the place. Peter, I can have the company plane in Salem in a couple of hours. Will you come to Seattle to talk with me about this?"

Chávez was stunned. A company plane. Haynes must have become a true drug mogul. "Michael, can we slow down for just a minute? I really want to help, but I don't know what I can do to help you or your son. I don't know anything about Russian law, nor do I know any Russian lawyers. You actually think there is some way I can help you?"

The weak raspy voice somehow grew louder. Some of the ghetto jive Chávez remembered from their first meeting inflected the delivery, "Look man, I know this seems completely out of the blue to you, crazy you know. Shit, everyone in the Northwest knows about you. You defended that Russian dickhead in Seattle. The guy that supposedly financed a whole fuckin' freighter of coke. I saw you on TV, and I read in the newspaper all about how you kicked the Feds' asses all over the courtroom. You speak Russian. I need you to defend my kid. Jonathan is not like me. He's a good kid, he works hard, never been in any trouble. Peter, I know I am asking a lot. At least come and talk to me."

Chávez's instinct for caution, preparation, and deliberateness warred against the answer he knew he was obligated to give.

"I will be at the Salem airport when your plane lands."

* * * * * * * * * *

Chávez barely noticed the luxurious interior of the Beechcraft twin turbo prop aircraft or the ride into downtown Seattle, lost in his thoughts about the past. He owed Michael Haynes his continued existence on earth.

Haynes Resources and Development occupied the thirtieth floor of the Orion Building. Entering the suite of offices Chávez wondered whether the business was legitimate or was some kind of money laundering front. Even if the business was legitimate, the proceeds of those drug sales likely were the foundation for the business. Chávez was directed to the conference room where his eyes instantly focused on Michael Haynes seated at the end of the long conference table. He was wearing an oxygen pack. A plastic tube stretched to his nostrils. Chávez was sure that his facial expression gave away his shock at Haynes' frail appearance. A woman and a man about the same age as Chávez and Haynes were seated across the table from Haynes.

Haynes slowly raised himself from his chair. He seemed to have shrunk significantly from the six foot four frame that Chávez remembered. His breathing was labored and raspy. The man facing Chávez no longer bore any resemblance to the powerful young black man that had left the safety of a bunker, risking his own life to save another soldier he had never even spoken to.

Haynes did not waste time. "Peter, I have congestive heart failure. I am dying. It's just a question of how long my heart will keep beating."

Chávez could not think of a response as he sat down in an empty chair. This time the jive and informality were absent.

Haynes performed the introductions. The man and woman at the table were lawyers from an international law firm. Haynes' personal lawyer had contacted them. Garrett, Hemann, and Robertson had offices all over the world, including the Russian Far East. Oswald (Oz) Young was the senior partner in the Seattle office. Anne Sprouse, also in the Seattle office, was a Russian law specialist. She had worked in the Garrett offices in Vladivostok on the Asian mainland and in Yuzhno-Sakhalinsk, the largest city on Sakhalin Island.

Chávez had never heard of the firm and had never met a lawyer who practiced international law. He studied each of their faces. As he did, Chávez fought the urge to classify them—pompous and patronizing—based solely on their looks and dress. He wondered if they had any inkling that their successful businessman client got his start peddling dope.

Haynes began. "Jonathan has been working as a petroleum engineer for ExxonMobil on a project on the northern part of Sakhalin Island. He was in Seattle for the Christmas holidays and left Seattle three days ago to return to Sakhalin. The Russians arrested him when he stepped off the plane in Sakhalin. They eventually called someone at ExxonMobil to let them know that he had been arrested. His boss on Sakhalin called me. The Russians have accused Jonathan of raping and murdering a young woman. I think she was a newspaper reporter. I don't know much more than that."

Chávez knew that what he was about to say should wait, that he should organize his thoughts first. Instead, the words simply tumbled out. "Michael, I am sorry about your son. Believe me, I am. I just don't know what I could do to help you or him."

Young and Sprouse looked at Chávez, then at Haynes. They said nothing, but Chávez could read their smug expressions. He had seen it before. These kinds of lawyers thought they were the center of the universe, dismissing any thought that a lawyer from a small city in Oregon actually might be able to compete in their arena, even one who had two victories in the United States Supreme Court. Chávez could feel the disorientation that he had experienced since he had answered Haynes' call begin to dissipate. The smug expressions portrayed by

Young and Sprouse were beginning to fuel his competitive juices.

"The U.S. Consulate office is in Vladivostok. They can provide support, but they can't interfere. There is nothing they can do." Haynes continued.

Chávez remained silent.

"May I call you Peter?" Young inquired.

"Sure," Chávez replied, leaving to himself his thoughts about the smug son of a bitch addressing him.

"Peter, let me give you some background on the Russian legal system. It might surprise you."

Chávez thought to himself, "Hell, I am in a mahogany paneled suite of offices with a drug dealer, transformed into a real estate magnate, who wants me to defend his son in the Russian Far East. Why would anything surprise me at this point?"

"Since '91, when the Soviet Union collapsed, the Russian Federation operates as a constitutional democracy. Criminal defendants charged with serious crimes now have the right to a jury trial."

"You said they have jury trials there. Do you know a criminal lawyer there?" Chávez asked, hoping that would begin his exodus from what was becoming the most bizarre and uncomfortable situation of his professional life.

Young looked over at Sprouse. "They have only had jury trials in the Russian Far East for a few years. There have only been a couple of jury trials in Sakhalin so far."

Young paused. Chávez assumed that the pause was to let him react to Young's last statement. Instead, Chávez nodded and continued to look directly at Young indicating that Young should continue.

"Sure, there are Russian lawyers with jury experience—some good ones in fact. There is a lawyer in our office on Sakhalin, Katya Osipova, who has had a jury trial. She defended a Russian ExxonMobil employee last year in Vladivostok. The jury acquitted him."

Haynes interjected, "Chávez, I can pay whatever you ask. Go there and defend my son."

Haynes' words struck Chávez like lightening bolts. He tried not to react outwardly. He owed Haynes a debt. Haynes now wanted it repaid. He tried to remain calm, make his voice steady.

"Michael, your confidence in me is humbling. I don't know Russian law or procedure. Even if I could learn it, they surely won't permit an American lawyer to appear in court there. Hell, it's likely that the presence of an American appearing on your son's behalf would hurt him. My presence alone might cause the Russians to over-react against him."

Young and Sprouse looked at Michael Haynes. Again their supercilious expressions said, "Mr. Haynes, we told you that this would be his reaction. What you want is not in your son's best interest."

Haynes spoke again. "Look, I am almost dead. Go and bring Jonathan home. I may not live to see it, but at least I will know that Jonathan's life is in your hands. I will have done all I could for the one good thing that I gave to this world. Peter, I actually prayed about this, and you're God's answer."

Chávez hesitated. He sensed every eye in the room directed at him. The words, "A drug dealer who prays," stayed well behind his lips. "Did you know I tried my last case three weeks ago? The president has nominated me for the U.S. District Court in Portland."

Chávez watched Haynes noticeably recoil, as if he had just been sucker punched in the gut.

"Shit, why do you want to be a judge? You've got to be making a ton of money. Maybe you could postpone putting on the robe for awhile?"

Chávez stood and walked to the window. Three pairs of eyes followed him. Puget Sound appeared cold and forbidding in the winter sunlight. His eyes, however, looked beyond the Sound, to the Pacific, to another time more than thirty years before. Involuntarily, he touched the raised red scar on his left wrist. Then he boomeranged back to the thirtieth floor of the Orion Building.

Thinking about taking the bench had helped him fight the loneliness and depression that periodically overtook him after Claire's death. The judgeship was in his grasp. Senator Garlock's words rang ominously in his head, "Anything controversial could put your nomination in jeopardy."

He could feel Claire's presence and hear her voice, cautioning him against the natural impetuousness that he often fought to control when he was younger. Then his Latin blood could rise in an instant. Almost from the beginning of their marriage, he had asked Claire's advice regarding cases about which he was unsure. That advice, usually cautioning him against taking a case, had been right every time. He sensed the soft touch of her hand brush across his face, focusing him, telling him, "No, it has been too long—Haynes is asking too much." But Claire was dead.

Perhaps he could have it both ways. Maybe it was all just a big mistake and the young man's case would resolve itself. At the worst he could go to Russia for a week, two at the most. Perhaps two weeks in Russia would be enough to repay the debt that he owed Michael Haynes. He turned from the window.

"I'll go as soon as I can."

CHAPTER

4

Masterkov sat across from the Prokuror General's large, rectangular desk. To prepare for the meeting, he had arranged the important parts of the investigative file across his lap. Masterkov generally feared no one; he was, however, wary of Yuri Karpov.

Karpov entered his office from a side door. He was an imposing man, over six feet tall and a muscular two hundred pounds. Dark haired, handsome and articulate, Karpov seemed destined for positions beyond that of Prokuror General of a small region in the remote Russian Far East. There was a combination of intellect and steeliness to Karpov that made Masterkov uneasy around him.

"Alexander Sergeevich, thank you for meeting me at such an early hour."

"Certainly, sir. I am usually at work by seven a.m. anyway."

"I know. You have always been diligent in your work during the five years that I have been here. My predecessor told me that it was that way when you worked for him.

"As you know, the press is making inquiries. It's personal with them. They think Sergova's murder was a contract hit like the murders of the other journalists around the country. They want to know the details of the Haynes case. How you knew he would return to Russia and the exact time he would return. You have to admit your methods appear to have been a bit out of the ordinary."

Masterkov did not react. However, the conversation was beginning in such a weird way. What the hell did Karpov mean about methods out of the ordinary? It was Karpov that pressured him to focus on Haynes as the sole suspect as soon as he learned about the fingerprint, even though Masterkov had wanted to go more slowly. Karpov had received his reports every step of the way. Masterkov continued to look directly at Karpov, relieved at some level that Karpov was focused on the investigation and seemingly knew nothing of Masterkov's close relationship to Sergova and her father.

Although Karpov's chief deputy, Andrey Barbatov, would handle the in-court day-to-day prosecution, the way the conversation had begun made it clear to Masterkov that Karpov was continuing to monitor the case closely. Masterkov was beginning to doubt that Karpov's interest was purely professional or motivated solely by the international press coverage, which would only increase as the case progressed. Many American oil workers had been charged with crimes in Yuzhno—though none as serious as murder. He assumed that, like most things in Russia, something below the surface was motivating Karpov's overly intense interest in every aspect of the case. Karpov had never before requested a conference like this one, no matter how serious the case.

"So, please start from the beginning. I need the important details."

"Yes, it's not that complicated. As you know from my reports, it started with the fingerprint. IAFIS matched the print on the wine glass in Sergova's apartment with Haynes. I assume, General, that you have read Popov's report?"

"Yes, yes, I have read the report," Karpov replied sharply, "I want to know what is not in your reports. How did you actually investigate Haynes without Exxon or Haynes finding out? That information is not in the investigative file."

Again, Masterkov was surprised by Karpov's directness. Karpov must have actually studied the investigative file closely. Was he just being thorough, was he trying to catch Masterkov in some illegality, or was there a deeper motive to Karpov's unusual interest? Did Karpov know that Masterkov always kept his own secret file?

"Who is Lyudmila Plotnikova?"

The question jarred Masterkov. Her name was not mentioned in any report. Yet, Karpov knew that he had talked to Lyudmila. Masterkov could feel Karpov's eyes boring in on him, as if Karpov was trying to see his inner thoughts. Masterkov did not hesitate.

"A personal acquaintance at Exxon-Neftgas."

"Why did you go to her about this?"

The fact that Karpov knew about Lyudmila meant he knew the answers to the questions that he was asking.

"Lyudmila works in human resources. I met her a couple of years ago when I investigated a break-in at the corporate offices. She has computer access to the Exxon-Mobil personnel records."

Quickly, Masterkov brought his contact with Lyud-mila to the front of his brain. The whole thing had been awkward. He and Lyudmila had been more than professional acquaintances, but that had ended more than a year ago. He assumed that she agreed to get him the information because either she still cared for him or she simply wanted to remain on his good side, knowing that Masterkov had the power to make her life difficult. He would not have done that, but he needed the information. Either she had told someone about what she had done, or she was wrong about her ability to access the computer records undetected. In any event, he needed to let her know that Karpov and likely others knew about her involvement in the case.

"Because Haynes is an American I assumed that he worked for one of the oil companies, and Exxon was the most likely. I also thought that, like most of the American oil workers, he had probably gone back to the U.S. for Christmas."

"Exactly what information did Plotnikova provide to you?"

"Just the essentials—that Haynes was a petroleum engineer. That he worked up in Nogliki. That he had gone home for Christmas and was due back in Nogliki on January 21st."

"How did you know he would return?"

"Electronic airline ticket records. General, the source is unimportant. I knew he had a return ticket. I suspect you know all this. You know I did it all in secret because we have no extradition treaty with the U.S. Had I contacted the U.S. FBI we might never have gotten him back, or it would have taken years."

"Yes, actually, it was brilliant. I just don't want any surprises when the American lawyer gets here."

"American lawyer? You already know that an American lawyer is coming? It's only been a few days since I took him into custody." Masterkov blurted out, surprised at his own unscripted response.

Masterkov was impressed, Karpov's own sources ran deep; perhaps Karpov's sources rivaled his own?

"Yes, it's an American lawyer, though not some famous celebrity lawyer. He's from the American west coast, a little state—Oregon. How I know is unimportant. He will arrive tomorrow. Is there anything I need to know before the international press starts crawling all over us? I want no surprises."

Surprises, Masterkov mused. Events in Russia were never without surprises. An American lawyer, what the hell could he do?

"No, there will be no surprises. The case is a lock. Haynes lied to me repeatedly about knowing Sergova and admitted to everything but placing his hands on her neck and strangling her. The fingerprint match is solid. We completed the DNA semen and hair match yesterday. It's Haynes' semen in Sergova's vagina. We have an eyewitness placing Haynes with Sergova at the 777 Club the night she was murdered. The 777 Club is a notorious meat market. The American oil workers go there to find a fuck for the night. The Russian women go there to find an American husband. There really aren't many six-foot-four black men on Sakhalin," Masterkov acknowledged sarcastically.

For the first time in the meeting Masterkov observed a slight smile appear on Karpov's face.

"Thank you, Alexander Sergeevich. We are counting on you. The world will be watching how our judicial system works."

Masterkov smiled back. "Yes, General. Everything is set."

CHAPTER

5

Chávez felt light-headed and even a bit unsteady as he walked down the jetway. He was headed for Seoul and then Sakhalin, Russia. In Haynes' office, when he agreed to go to Sakhalin, Chávez had thought in the back of his mind that the moment likely would never arrive. Something or someone would intervene to spare him. Since leaving Haynes' office in Seattle, a sense of dread, a sense that he was making a catastrophic mistake, greeted him every morning when he awoke. Yet, he owed Michael Haynes his life.

Chávez had assumed that getting a visa would be difficult. He even hoped that he might be denied a visa, particularly if the Russian authorities knew why he wanted to enter their country. In the event that he was denied a visa, there would be nothing he could do, and his conscience would be clear. Instead, the visa was issued two weeks after the meeting in Seattle, no doubt due to the Garrett firm's international connections. Chávez and Haynes had not directly discussed a fee. Given the extraordinary debt he owed Haynes, Chávez thought it was possible that Haynes expected him to take the case pro bono. However, a cashier's check for $350,000 with the promise of more if needed arrived by FedEx right after the visa. The check remained in the office safe. Chávez continued to tell himself that he would be back home in a week or two. The March date for his appearance in Washington, D.C. before the Senate Judiciary Committee remained in bold text on his electronic calendar. Senator Garlock was a bit taken aback when Chávez informed him of his involvement in the case that was gaining some international notoriety. Garlock calmed down, however, when Chávez explained the bond that connected him to the Haynes' case. Chávez assured him that his stay in Russia would be brief.

After settling into his business class seat and ordering a Bombay Sapphire martini, Chávez removed two manila envelopes from his briefcase. Sprouse had given him a thick one at the airport in Seattle. Chávez's investigator, Tom McCallum, had given him the other one just before Chávez left Salem.

Who was Michael Haynes, and who was his son? He opened McCallum's envelope first. Immediately, the strong suspicions that he had harbored about Michael Haynes for more than 30 years were confirmed. McCallum, an ex-FBI agent who still had close contacts within the FBI, had pieced together enough information from two-decade-old records to establish that indeed Haynes began selling drugs soon after he returned from Vietnam. It was likely that Haynes had established himself in the business while a soldier in Vietnam. The drug career had lasted about a decade and a half. During that time Haynes began buying commercial property and then became a developer, transforming cash stained with heroin, cocaine, and marijuana into a real estate empire. Although Haynes was in the FBI's and the DEA's records, identified as a suspected drug kingpin, there had never been enough evidence to attempt a prosecution. Haynes Resources and Development now owned well over $600 million in commercial properties from Seattle to Los Angeles. Michael Haynes was the sole owner. Whoever was Jonathan Haynes' mother had long since disappeared.

Jonathan Haynes had obtained his chemical engineering degree from a Midwest university, attending the university on a basketball scholarship following a great high school basketball career at Seattle Prep. Typical of McCallum, he had left the name of the university out of the official report on the chance it might be seen by the opposition. McCallum had traveled to the university to see if he could learn a little more about Jonathan Haynes. McCallum's report began with easily obtainable information—basketball (though only a part-time starter), decent grades, arrested for a minor disturbance following a football game, no formal charges filed. Jonathan Haynes had lived in a small men's dorm—a so-called jock dorm on the northwest end of the campus. Chávez wondered where McCallum was going with information about the dorm where Jonathan Haynes resided during his college years. He sensed the destination wasn't good and turned the page.

There it was. During his junior year Jonathan Haynes had been accused of rape by a young coed from Florida. The university investigation established that the girl was very drunk and had gone with Jonathan and some other athletes to the dorm. She gave conflicting stories about who was involved and to what extent she had consented to sexual contact. The young woman accused Jonathan Haynes of forcing her to have sexual intercourse with him. Interestingly, Jonathan Haynes was the only African American involved in the incident. Jonathan admitted bringing her back to the dorm, but he denied the girl's claim that he had had sexual intercourse with her. The school imposed some minor discipline. But that was it. No criminal charges had been filed. Chávez wondered why Jonathan had not been expelled over the incident. Perhaps Michael Haynes had made a large donation to the school.

Chávez felt a wave of anxiety wash over him as he contemplated the university incident. What were the chances that Jonathan Haynes was the victim of two false accusations? Chávez returned McCallum's report to the envelope. An American prosecutor would likely have the information about the incident, though Chávez doubted that the evidence would be admissible in an American courtroom. Nevertheless, he wondered whether the Russians had the investigative capacity to discover the incident.

He opened the packet from Sprouse. Inside were various articles, taken mostly from the Internet. Included were articles on Russia since the breakup of the Soviet Union, articles on Russian criminal law and procedure, and articles detailing Russia's vast oil and gas reserves being developed off the coast of Sakhalin. To Chávez's complete surprise one of the articles on the

Russian criminal procedure code was written by an Oregon Supreme Court justice who had spent a good deal of time in the Russian Far East. Chávez decided to begin with articles on the history of Sakhalin Island and Sakhalin's six multinational oil and gas ventures, move on to Russian criminal law and procedure, and finally the general articles on the so-called "New Russia."

Sakhalin Island had a sordid history. It had been a place of exile and prison since the time of the czars. The famous Russian playwright Anton Chekhov, a medical doctor by education and training, had traveled across the breadth of Russia to Sakhalin in the late 1890s and had spent a year chronicling the miserable lives of the island's inhabitants, including the prisoners chained to wheelbarrows twenty-four hours a day. During the Russo-Japanese war in the early 1900s, the Japanese had sunk nearly every ship in the Russian Navy in and around the Tatar Straits, the body of water separating the island from the Asian mainland. The Japanese had controlled the island until the end of World War II when the Russians finally had driven them out. No treaty was ever signed between the two countries, and they continued to contest some of the world's most productive fishing grounds associated with the ownership of the Kuril Islands, a series of islands stretching northwest from Sakhalin. After regaining control of the island in 1946, the Soviets designated the island a closed area, forbidding any entry by foreigners. The island remained that way until 1991. Despite the tremendous economic development associated with the six multinational oil and gas ventures, Sakhalin Island remained Russia's poorest region.

The Constitution of the Russian Federation, adopted by popular vote in 1993, established an adversarial system of criminal justice. Judges were supposed to be independent, and the prosecutor and the defendant equal before the court. There were, however, remnants of the old Soviet inquisitorial system that remained part of Russia's new criminal justice system. Even under the new so-called adversarial system, the prosecutor's office prepared an investigative file containing all of the investigative reports—witness interviews, expert reports, etc.—and those reports went to the judge, regardless of their content. Although the Russian Constitution guaranteed a jury trial for certain serious crimes, there were very few jury trials. The system seemed to operate much like it had during Soviet times. Most of the cases were tried to a judge or a panel of judges. Prosecutors were feared, the defense seldom put up a fight, and judges did what the prosecutors wanted, convicting 99 percent of the criminal defendants. Defendants who actually opted for a jury trial in front of twelve Russian citizens generally fared much better.

The Kremlin had used the courts to go after Russia's largest private oil company, Yukos, and its president, Mikhail Khodorkovsky. Khodorkovsky, one of Russia's so-called "oligarchs," had funded anti-Kremlin movements and failed to heed warnings to leave the country. The government now controlled all of Yukos' assets, and Khodorkovsky, once identified as one of the richest men in the world, was in a Russian prison for nine years. In every kind of case, judges were under extreme pressure to side with the government.

Even after the breakup of the Soviet Union, the Russian Federation remained the world's largest country, having more natural resources than any country in the world, one-fifth of the world's precious metals, one-third of the world's natural gas, and an estimated 17 to 25 percent of the world's oil. Despite its vast energy wealth, there remained throughout the country criminality and corruption, crumbling infrastructure and housing, a run-down health care system, and the highest rate of HIV outside of Africa. A survey revealed that Russian businesses and individuals had paid a combined three billion dollars in bribes the year before, eclipsing the amount paid to the central government in taxes. The wife of the mayor of Moscow had made the Forbes list as the eighth richest woman in Europe with a net worth of more than four billion dollars. Despite a constitution granting more rights and privileges to Russian citizens than did the American constitution, Russia was mired in corruption from top to bottom.

Two hours after leaving Seoul, Sakhalin Island came into view. Rugged snow-covered peaks and forests were framed by frozen ocean. Although everything was snow-covered and frozen, nothing was actually white; instead, everything had a gray cast to it. Older broken-down military helicopters could be seen as the plane taxied to the terminal. Chávez had a hard time believing that it was from this airfield that the Russian MIGs had been scrambled to shoot down KAL flight 54. The whole place seemed forbidding, old, and in need of structural repairs and paint.

Chávez had to walk at least a hundred yards across the frozen snow-covered tarmac to the international terminal. Although it was about three in the afternoon nothing was melting. Chávez estimated the temperature at ten degrees Fahrenheit. His whole body shook from the cold as he walked to the terminal.

Chávez tried to appear congenial and confident as he approached the immigration counter. The grim-looking woman behind the counter squeezed her eyes nearly closed as if to focus more closely on Chávez's face. The stench of stale cigarette smoke formed an invisible screen around her. Chávez had received a number of emails from Yekaterina Osipova, the lawyer in the Garrett firm representing Jonathan since his arrest. He had been looking forward to seeing the face behind the short but informative emails, signed Katya. He desperately hoped that the woman with whom he would be working bore no resemblance to the stern wrinkle-faced woman who now confronted him at the immigration counter. That woman ignored his friendly Russian hello. Quickly she snatched the passport from his outstretched right hand and began to pound her computer keyboard. After what seemed to be an eternity, she raised her squinty eyes from the computer screen. Instead of handing Chávez's passport back to him, she locked her eyes on a nearby border guard still dressed in a Soviet-style uniform. The guard immediately approached the immigration counter.

CHAPTER

6

The airline source that enabled Masterkov to meet Jonathan Haynes' arriving flight had provided the same accurate information on Chávez's flight plan from the U.S. After meeting with immigration officials and the border guards on duty, Masterkov, wearing civilian clothes, had partially hidden himself in an alcove. From there he could see most of the terminal without being observed. Within minutes he had spotted two of Karpov's operatives lurking in the terminal. Katya Osipova had arrived about fifteen minutes after Masterkov and was waiting near the immigration exit door.

Masterkov had first seen Katya Osipova on Sakhalin about four years earlier, just as ExxonMobil had begun to increase its administrative staff on the island. Eventually, Masterkov learned that Osipova worked for one of the international law firms that represented ExxonMobil in its oil and gas dealings on the island. He also learned that she had been a prosecutor at one time in her legal career. And he knew about the unfortunate events in Vladivostok that ultimately brought her to Sakhalin.

Not long after his wife Irina had left him and completed their long-anticipated divorce, Masterkov began speaking to Osipova on her frequent appearances at the Prokuror's office. Their conversations were always pleasant but centered on their adversarial business. Now, as he watched her prepare to meet Chávez, he regretted not having attempted to move the relationship to a different level.

Masterkov suppressed a smile as he thought about how the American would react to the gorgeous Russian lawyer. Had she chosen the knee length boots, the white three-quarter length fur coat and matching fur hat with some care, knowing that the media would be present to record her first meeting with the American lawyer? Conscious or not, the effect was striking. Every man in the terminal glanced more than once in Osipova's direction.

When Katya Osipova had contacted the Prokuror's office soon after Haynes' arrest, Masterkov had thought it likely that, despite Osipova's talents and experience, her firm would send another Exxon lawyer to help with the case. However, Masterkov assumed that should that occur, the lawyer would be one of Exxon's white-gloved oil and gas lawyers, the kind of lawyer used to capitulating to the Russian government in energy negotiations. Even an American lawyer would not be unprecedented. Mikhail Khodorkovsky's defense team had included a well-known American lawyer, though he was never permitted to sit on the other side of the bar with the defense team, nor was he allowed to participate officially in any court proceedings.

Chávez, however, was not the kind of lawyer Masterkov had expected. As soon as he had left Karpov's office, Masterkov had done a Google search on Chávez. The results were interesting. Three things had captured Masterkov's attention. First, Chávez was not what the media might describe as a nationally recognized lawyer. That was too bad. Everything Masterkov had learned about the American criminal defense lawyers with so-called national reputations was that they lost most of their cases. It was Masterkov's opinion that the current cadre of "famous" American criminal defense lawyers were mediocre at best. Lawyers like Chávez, lawyers that had great local reputations, seemed to be the most dangerous in American courtrooms. To Masterkov the O.J. Simpson case was the best illustration. No one outside of Los Angeles had ever heard of Johnnie Cochran.

Masterkov feared that Chávez was one of those Johnnie Cochran type lawyers, particularly after Masterkov had found a series of articles from the *Seattle Post Intelligencer* detailing Chávez's successful defense of a Russian drug kingpin, Ilya Padchin. Padchin had been accused in the U.S. District Court in Seattle of masterminding a wide-ranging drug conspiracy that smuggled massive amounts of drugs into the U.S. on freighters that Padchin owned through a series of offshore corporations. According to the newspaper reports, Chávez's cross-examination of the government's key Russian witnesses made the witnesses look like complete fools. Some of the jurors shook their heads, rolled their eyes, and laughed as the prosecutor tried to rehabilitate the witnesses on redirect examination. Although there were Russian interpreters in the courtroom to translate the English questions and the Russian answers, Chávez often asked questions to witnesses directly in Russian, which often seemed to unnerve the Russian witnesses or cause them to agree with propositions that devastated the government's case at every turn. The acquittal in that case had taken less than four hours of jury deliberation.

Masterkov found Chávez a bit puzzling, however, at least from the research that was available. The U.S. president had nominated Chávez for a position on the U.S. District Court in Oregon. The nomination was not without controversy, however, because of Chávez's successful criminal defense practice. Apparently, the evangelicals and right-wing Republicans were hostile to the nomination. Chávez's confirmation hearing was scheduled for late March. Why had Chávez been retained, and what would motivate Chávez to risk such a prestigious end-of-career opportunity to become involved in the defense of some unknown oil worker on a remote island in the Russian Far East?

Although Osipova seemed outwardly at ease, Masterkov was certain that she was becoming a bit anxious. The steady stream of passengers coming through the immigration and customs exit had ceased. The plane had been on the ground for more than an hour. She had to assume Chávez was being put through some difficulty, an assumption that Masterkov knew was well founded.

As Masterkov pondered the activities of the border guards and customs officers that he had set in motion, the exit door opened. He had seen Mexican and Latin American men in American movies and had assumed that Chávez would somehow resemble the Mexicans he had seen in those films—the ones that lived in villages in American cowboy movies. This man was much different. His complexion was dark but not brown. From the Internet articles Masterkov believed that Chávez was in his late fifties or even sixty. This man, however, with his high cheek-bones and the prominent aquiline nose of the Spanish nobility, appeared younger and in excellent physical shape. His straight hair, combed back and parted on the left, was still black but with streaks of gray on the sides. More importantly to Masterkov, the American lawyer seemed completely unfazed by the intensive inspection of his personal things that Masterkov had arranged. Nor did the man seem intimidated in the slightest by the media onslaught. As Masterkov watched Chávez deftly answer the reporters' questions, he contemplated whether Chávez's apparent confidence would remain after he had reviewed the contents of the investigative file and experienced firsthand the judicial system of the so-called "New Russia."

CHAPTER

7

C hávez's immediate and intense physical attraction to the beautiful Russian woman now walking from the terminal with him in the freezing cold erased all the irritation he had just experienced with the squinty-eyed, cigarette-smoke smelling immigration official and the border guard who questioned him intensely about his business in Russia, examining every personal item in his suitcases and briefcase as if he was unfamiliar with a razor, shoes, and other personal items. The sensation he was now experiencing, he recalled only slightly from his youth. He found it unnerving. Katya was tall, about five foot nine, with the blonde, blue-eyed Nordic look associated with Russians from the northwestern reaches of the country. Chávez surmised that Katya was likely fifteen years younger than he. Although she was wearing a three-quarter length white fur coat, Chávez could tell that underneath the coat was a trim and beautifully proportioned body. Each time she glanced at him as they conversed in basic Russian, Katya's deep blue eyes seemed to sparkle even in the gray afternoon light and dirty snow and ice that surrounded them in the terminal parking lot.

Having deposited his bags in the back of Katya's Toyota Land Cruiser, Chávez started for the left front of the car to open Katya's driver side door for her. She, however, went to the right front of the car. Embarrassed, he realized that he had failed to notice that the steering wheel was located on the right hand side of the car.

As Chávez slid into the front passenger seat he immediately encountered the scent of vanilla. He assumed that that scent emanated from a small round canister attached by a magnet to the dash. However, almost instantly vanilla gave way to an obvious perfume scent. Chávez doubted he had smelled the perfume before, but found it very pleasing. Again, the sensations that seemed to be awakening in him were unsettling. More unsettling perhaps was the fact that, although Russians in the Far East steered their cars from the right, they also drove on the right side of the road.

Chávez read the signs as Katya maneuvered the Toyota from the terminal parking lot onto the road toward the city. Although Chávez had answered the media questions in Russian, he was not completely confident that his answers had demonstrated the fluency with the language that he had hoped to portray. Chávez was, however, confident that his fluency would soon return. The army's Russian language school in Monterey, California, had been excellent. He was fluent in Russian when he left the school headed for Vietnam. He had not, however, used his Russian language skills in Vietnam and only intermittently as a lawyer. He had taken a quick Russian refresher course just before the Padchin trial, and it had served him well in that case.With each sign his recognition seemed to speed up.

In perfect English, Katya broke what had become an awkward silence.

"Mr. Chávez, coming up on the right there is the American Village where many of the American oil workers reside."

Her English astonished him.

"Katya, please call me Peter. Your English is impeccable. Have you been to America?" Chávez replied a bit self-consciously, thinking of his very simple Russian replies to her initial greeting in the terminal.

"Yes, I studied on a Marshall scholarship at the law school at the University of Michigan. Actually, I have an LLM in international law from the law school."

Chávez suppressed the urge to say, "That's amazing, what are you doing in this far corner of the world?" Instead, he asked, "When was that?" thinking that her answer might also help him determine her age.

"In 1988 and '89, immediately after I completed my law studies at Moscow State University," Katya replied.

Chávez remembered that, unlike in America, a legal education in Europe and Russia generally occurred at the undergraduate level, taking five years. He was now confident that she was in her early forties.

Glancing to his right, Chávez saw a clash of cultures, East versus West, as the forlorn-looking Russian buildings and rows of dilapidated Soviet-style cinderblock apartments gave way to a gated community of modern duplexes and well-maintained grounds. A large sign above the gate identified the American Village.

In an instant the landscape returned again to what Chávez could only describe as a state of disrepair.

Although he did not want to offend Katya, Chávez decided to risk a question about the city's run-down condition.

"Katya, on the way over I read that the oil and gas projects have brought more than a hundred billion dollars to this region. Are local Russians benefiting from the investment?"

Although Katya kept her eyes on the road ahead, Chávez could see her facial muscles tense slightly at his statement.

"Well, that's an interesting question." Katya replied in English. "Average Russians should be benefiting from the oil and gas projects. We are the largest country in the world—we have the most natural resources in the world. Much of the world's oil and gas is right here." Then gesturing toward another run-down apartment building to her left, she said, "But you see how the average Russian lives here in the Far East."

"I hope my comment did not offend you. I didn't mean to," Chávez interjected, feeling that he might have gone too far in their very first meeting.

"No, I understand completely," Katya replied.

From his reading on the way over Chávez recalled that Japan's northernmost island, Hokkaido, was only sixty-four miles to the south and that the Japanese had occupied Sakhalin Island between 1905 and the end of World War II. As a result Chávez had expected to see an Asian influence on the city's architecture. However, the only thing Japanese was the name on the hotel they stopped in front of—Sapporo.

Katya accompanied Chávez into the hotel. Although the outside of the hotel was indistinguishable from the other unimaginative and crumbling soviet-style buildings that dominated the city, the inside of the hotel seemed warm and inviting, particularly the bar.

Chávez had no trouble following Katya's conversation conducted in rapid Russian with the unsmiling desk clerk. Chávez needed to surrender his passport; the clerk would register him as a guest in the city.

Chávez balked. "You mean I have to give them my passport?" he asked Katya in irritated English.

Katya smiled and answered in English. "Yes, Peter, it is standard procedure. All foreign visitors must be registered. They will keep your passport in the hotel safe, so there will be no danger of it being stolen from you while you are here."

Registration, stolen passports—he was now in a different world. Reluctantly, Chávez removed his passport from the breast pocket of his sport coat and handed it to the desk clerk.

With the hotel check-in complete, Katya again spoke in English.

"You will find your room small by American standards. However, it will be nicely furnished, and there will be an Internet hook-up in the room. I am sure you are tired. I will pick you up at eight tomorrow morning. The Detention Center is only two blocks from here. They will let us see Mr. Haynes then. I have written my cell number on my card."

Chávez took the card and then clasped her hand with both of his. He spoke in Russian.

"Thank you, Katya. I look forward to working with you. Mr. Haynes is fortunate that you are here."

Her hand was warm; her eyes sparkled. Chávez felt something very genuine in the smile that she returned.

Inside the room Chávez connected his laptop to the Ethernet cord and accessed his email. The first new message was from Anne Sprouse, the Seattle lawyer in Katya's firm. The message was straightforward. Michael Haynes had died of congestive heart failure a few hours after Chávez had boarded the plane for Seoul. There would be no funeral. The Sakhalin Detention Center had been contacted, and Jonathan Haynes was informed of his father's death.

Chávez continued to stare at the computer screen. Michael Haynes was dead. Chávez owed the father, but what did he owe the son? He looked over at his unpacked suitcase. He could be home in forty-eight hours, devoting all of his time and energy to becoming Oregon's first Hispanic federal judge.

But did a debt, one forged by blood, disappear because the creditor died? The answer was an unequivocal no. This debt was renewed everyday that Chávez got out of bed. Michael Haynes' blood flowed through the body of the young man locked in the Detention Center a couple of blocks away. Chávez got up from the chair, walked over to his suitcase, and unsnapped the clasp.

As he unpacked Chávez turned on the radio. The disc jockey's voice had a mechanical high-pitched quality to it. He pictured a character from *Mad Magazine* as the face behind the voice. Just after hanging up his suits he heard the names Haynes and Chávez, and for the first time, a description of the brutal rape and murder of Olga Sergova. He was accustomed to fighting the government with all of its might arrayed against a client. But, in America, the Constitution and a well-selected jury helped to even the odds. The reality that Jonathan Haynes may not have any of those protections struck him hard; he might fail. Everything that his professional life stood for could end poorly on a remote island in the Russian Far East. He began to feel nauseated and laid down on the bed. His leg and back muscles ached. As he closed his eyes his thoughts drifted through the past.

His grandmother had disapproved of his mother's marriage to a "Mexican" as she described his father and had refused to attend the wedding. His grandmother cared less that his father had earned a Silver and a Bronze star in World War II and was descended from an old-line New Mexico family that had owned land in New Mexico before the Gadsden Purchase. Chávez's young mother eventually gave into his grandmother's unrelenting pressure. The marriage ended soon after Chávez was born. His mother had returned with him to Portland and the security of her parents' home. As it turned out, none of it mattered much. His father had died a few years later, possibly never truly recovering from his war wounds. Despite his grandmother's attitude toward Chávez's father, she and his grandfather adored him.

Chávez sensed the patient glance of his long-dead grandfather, the only father he had ever known. His grandfather had taught him to read when he was four years old, guiding him through *Treasure Island*, *Robinson Crusoe*, and all of the Alexander Dumas books. It was his grandfather who taught him to swing a baseball bat, throw a football, and punch back hard when it was necessary. His grandfather was the man who had instilled in him the belief that you should never go back on your word, and that inner strength and character were not strangers to understanding and compassion. Chávez knew that often it had been his capacity for understanding and compassion, imprinted by his grandfather on him at a young age, that had helped him form a bond of trust with some of his most difficult clients—clients who had done unspeakable things. More so than ever in his life, Chávez realized that he would need all of his strength and all of his intellect to have any chance of successfully navigating the Russian legal system.

Most nights as sleep approached, Chávez would think about Claire, wanting to dream and experience again a feeling of contentment—to sense again the security and the warmth of Claire's body intertwined with his as they had drifted off to sleep together. Now, thousands of miles from all that was familiar, Chávez hoped that those same feelings of contentment would find him during his first night in Russia. He wanted, if ever so briefly, to be free from the nagging feeling that he had made a mistake that could cost him a federal judgeship.

CHAPTER

8

A t six-thirty a.m. Masterkov entered the Detention Center through a service entrance. The commandant of the center had not questioned Masterkov's request for access to the prisoner interview room and left him alone in the room immediately upon opening the door. From his briefcase Masterkov removed two tiny sound-sensing devices. He placed one of the devices inside the side edge of the small table located in the middle of the room. The other he placed under the metal cover that protected a light protruding from one of the walls. Satisfied that the bugs could not be detected even under careful scrutiny, Masterkov withdrew to a small room a few doors down from the prisoner interview room to await Chávez's arrival.

Comfortably seated in the room, Masterkov warmed his hands on a large cup of tea that he had poured from an old silver thermos. Next he adjusted the receiver of the wireless recording device he had placed on the table in front of him. Masterkov had used the device twice before to listen to the conversations between lawyers and their clients. Those occasions involved American oil workers charged in a drug conspiracy. Although he had bugged the conversations, it was not to obtain more evidence against the Americans. Instead, he wanted to learn everything he possibly could about other conspirators and what organization was at the center of the conspiracy. The information he had obtained from that eavesdropping had proved invaluable in his successful efforts in destroying a drug smuggling and distribution conspiracy masterminded by the Japanese Mafia in a network that stretched from Tokyo to Seoul to Sakhalin. He had never listened in on a conversation between a Russian defendant and Russian lawyer, mostly because the Russian lawyers appointed to represent criminal defendants rarely visited their clients and rarely ever spent any time preparing to adequately represent their clients in court—the state-paid compensation was just too low. He knew it was wrong to bug, completely contrary to the concept of a fair adversarial system that the new Russian Constitution mandated. Nevertheless, he had convinced himself that the Haynes case was just too important not to know more about it than anyone else.

A little before eight he heard the door to the prisoner interview room open. He estimated that the temperature in the room was about four degrees Celsius. Jonathan Haynes began coughing as soon as he entered. Masterkov was sure Haynes was suffering from some severe type of respiratory problem and likely had lost about fifteen pounds since his incarceration in the Detention Center. Guards had checked on Haynes every half hour after the commandant of the Center had informed Haynes that his father had died. The commandant had reported that Haynes had teared up when he first received the news. After that initial reaction, Haynes had simply laid down on his cot and stared at the ceiling until the early morning hours when he appeared to fall asleep.

Amnesty International had issued numerous reports about the deplorable conditions in the pretrial detention centers throughout Russia. The Detention Center on Sakhalin was no different. A number of prisoners undergoing lengthy pretrial incarceration had contracted tuberculosis and other serious diseases. Karpov seemed oblivious to the dangerous health conditions in the Detention Center. For many Russians, it was a death sentence before trial. Masterkov was sure that the Amnesty International people would show up as the international press started devoting more coverage to the Haynes case.

Haynes's coughing fit assured Masterkov that the wireless recording device was working properly. The device was so good that Masterkov could hear the guards move the chair back from the table and then instruct Haynes to sit in the chair.

CHAPTER

9

Chávez had interviewed clients and witnesses in jails throughout the Pacific Northwest. Although the jails varied in age, size, and shape, there was a similarity to them. They were stark, well lit, and smelled mostly of a combination of disinfectant, urine, and body odor. The instant he entered the Yuzhno Detention Center, a rancid smell he could not identify overwhelmed him. Katya, however, seemed unaffected. The odor that assaulted his nostrils was ever-present as the jailers conducted the inevitable pat down of his body and a complete search of the contents of his briefcase. Those preliminaries out of the way, Chávez and Katya were led to a small room at the end of a dim hallway. As they entered the freezing room, the rancid smell changed a bit, seemingly combined with a wet moldy smell that emanated from the old linoleum floor and peeling plaster walls.

During the short ride from the hotel, Katya informed Chávez that she had talked to a contact inside the Detention Center about how Haynes had reacted on learning about his father's death. According to Katya,

Haynes had little outward reaction, at least nothing that caused the guards to take notice.

Jonathan Haynes stood up from the table as soon as Chávez and Katya entered. As Chávez expected having read McCallum's report, Haynes was tall like his father, at least six foot four. He was also very dark like his father, but better looking, with a slight resemblance to the actor Will Smith. Chávez could not help wondering whether the young man standing before him had any inkling how his father first made his fortune. A wrinkled sweater and pants hung loosely on Haynes' lanky frame.

Katya began, "Jonathan, I am so sorry about your father. I am sure that he loved you very much. I told you that your father thought the most important thing he could do for you in the time he had left was to make sure that Mr. Chávez would come here to see what he could do to help you. He accomplished that, Jonathan. This is Peter Chávez."

Chávez extended his hand, "Jonathan, I am very sorry about your father."

Haynes did not speak in response. Instead he continued to look directly at Chávez, his eyes revealing a reticence—something less than complete acceptance. Nevertheless his handshake was firm.

"Jonathan I think you may know that your father saved my life in Vietnam. I owed him, so now I owe you."

Again, Jonathan Haynes said nothing in response.

"Jonathan, I think the first thing I need to know is whether you want to me to work on your case, to be your lawyer, at least to the extent that I can in this country.

Finally, Jonathan Haynes spoke. "I am okay with that. I know my father loved me, at least to the extent that he was capable of that emotion. Mr. Chávez, although my father tried to keep it from me, I know how my father first made his money. He had been a drug dealer. It is even possible that he was responsible for my mother's disappearance when I was a baby. But he was good to me. And yes, I am thankful that you are here. My father talked about you when I was growing up. A couple of years ago he sent me articles from the Seattle papers about some case where you defended some Russian mafia guy. My father was proud of saving your life. In some way, he felt a personal sense of pride in the success that you have made of your life. He said that despite your different lives there was an unbreakable connection between the two of you. He also said you were a good man, a good man like the fathers of some of my good friends in high school and at college. So yes, I am thankful you are here, but honestly I don't think there is much of anything you can do for me. I am a dead man already. Do you have any idea how corrupt this place is? They have decided to claim that I killed Olga, and they will do anything they want to do to see that they convict me. The only thing that might stop them is if I get TB or some other disease in here and die before the trial. Who knows, the way that I feel, I might already have something serious."

It seemed to Chávez that Jonathan had more to say, but a coughing spasm overtook him. As Jonathan coughed Chávez assessed the young man in front of him. He seemed to be an interesting combination. He was aware of his father's background, but he might as well have been some middle-class white kid. Chávez could tell Jonathan Haynes was likable. Chávez also immediately concluded that there was an authentic quality to Jonathan Haynes. Chávez suspected that when he eventually saw Jonathan smile it would be a broad one like his father's.

When Jonathan's coughing subsided, Chávez said, "Okay, Jonathan, then let's get started."

Jonathan simply nodded a reply.

"Is this some complete case of mistaken identity, or were you with Sergova the night before you left for the states? Do we need to challenge the scientific evidence?"

"Yes, I was with Olga," Jonathan replied in a barely audible voice.

"Okay, so it's your semen, your sperm, your pubic hair, and your DNA," Chávez stated, basing that assertion on Katya's claim that a source inside the Prokuror's office said they had such evidence.

"Yes, I guess so," Jonathan said looking down at the floor.

"Well, okay then, tell me the whole story about you and Olga Sergova."

Jonathan closed his eyes for an instant, as if to get the picture in his head. Then he began.

"I met Olga about six months ago. I came down from Nogliki where I work to Yuzhno for a meeting in the main office here. Some of the other guys had to get back, so the plane went back without me. I had to spend the night. I stayed at the Santa Hotel."

Chávez remembered that Katya had mentioned the Santa Hotel on the ride in. It was on the edge of the city toward the local ski area. She had considered having him stay there. However, she explained that she had opted for the Sapporo because it was in the heart of the city and closer to things.

Chávez interjected, "So how did you meet?"

"Well, it was summer, July. The Santa is actually at the north end of Yuri Gagarin Park here in Yuzhno. I decided to go for a run in the park before it got dark. About a mile into the run, I saw a woman on the trail. She was bending over, rubbing her ankle. I stopped. I tried to ask her in Russian if she needed help. My Russian wasn't perfect, but she spoke English. I could tell immediately she was frightened. To reassure her, I asked if she had a cell phone or wanted to use mine to call someone. She used mine and punched in a number but got no answer. I told her not to worry, I would be happy to walk her out of the park. Although she had turned her ankle, she could hobble with the help of a large stick that I found. It got dark before we reached her apartment. I told her I was an American engineer working for ExxonMobil and that I lived up in Nogliki. She told me that she was a reporter working for *Sovietsky Sakhalin*. I said goodbye to her at the outside entrance to her apartment."

As Jonathan paused Chávez said, "So that was in July. What happened next?"

"You mean, did I see Olga again?"

"Sure," Chávez replied.

"About a week later, I got a card from her at the project in Nogliki. She thanked me for the help and had written her cell phone number on the card. The next day, I called her."

"Jonathan, do you have that card? Is it someplace where we can get to it?"

"I am not really sure. It might still be in my flat in Nogliki."

Chávez glanced over at Katya. Her expression made it clear to Chávez that she understood the significance of the card. There was more to Jonathan's relationship with Olga Sergova than the night she was murdered.

Katya responded to Chávez's glance, "Peter, I went to Jonathan's flat in Nogliki the day after our firm was contacted. I am sure the *militsiya* had already searched it. There was not much left in the apartment. In fact, I suspect that after it was searched by the *militsiya*, someone else got in and took what was left or *vice versa*. There was no card in any drawer; everything was gone."

Chávez got the message. Things are different in Russia. The orderly way things worked in the American criminal justice system was not present in Russia.

"Go on," Chávez continued, trying not to show his concern about the loss of the card.

"Yes, I had to return to Yuzhno again in early August. I called her, and we agreed to meet for Korean food at the Holiday Restaurant on Lenin Street."

Inside Chávez chuckled. Lenin Street, how parochial. But then he thought about his own hometown, Portland, and its streets and high schools named Washington, Lincoln, and Grant. Maybe the Russian and the American people weren't so different.

"Then you must have been seen there," Chávez said, thinking to himself, how many six-foot-four black men can there be in Yuzhno? Particularly in the company of what Katya had described as a beautiful young Russian woman.

"Uh huh, I think so."

Chávez again glanced at Katya. Her look was the same. It said, "Perhaps, but don't count on it." Chávez suspected that even in the New Russia, Russians wanted to avoid any contact with the government if they could.

Katya interjected, "The Holiday Restaurant is one of the largest in Yuzhno. It serves different cuisines in different sections of the restaurant. The Korean section has mostly private dining cubicles."

"What happened after dinner that night?"

Jonathan's eyes seemed to brighten some more. "We talked a lot at dinner. The night was warm. We decided to walk back to her apartment. I left her again at the main door to her apartment building. She called a cab for me on her cell phone because I was staying at the Santa, and it was too far to walk."

Chávez cut in, "So again, you did not go into her apartment. Why not?"

"Well, she did not invite me that time. I did the next time."

"So tell us about the next time," Chávez replied.

There was a slight pause before Jonathan began again.

"We talked often on the phone during September. I was working hard, a lot of hours on the project, and I had no opportunity to go to Yuzhno either for work or just to see Olga. In October, I finally got a couple of days off. I took the train down, and this time I stayed at the Sapporo Hotel."

Chávez cut in, "By the way, do you have some close friends on the job? Did you tell any of them about seeing Olga?" Chávez asked.

"Sure. I think I told a couple of the other engineers that I was seeing someone in Yuzhno, but I am not sure I mentioned her name. I work with two other engineers, Rick Haselton and Tom Balmer. You could contact them."

Chávez wrote their names down and then returned to the narrative. "So, I assume you made arrangements to meet."

"Yes, Olga invited me for dinner at her apartment. I got there at about six p.m., I guess. It was a great evening. Olga cooked sturgeon that someone had given her. You know, we had a great time together. We did have some serious conversations though. She asked me about being black and if I dated white women in America. She asked me if I had had any trouble on Sakhalin because she thought that racial prejudice existed all over Russia, and there had been some incidents on Sakhalin. I told her I had friends of every color in America, and that, so far, so good—no real problems on Sakhalin." Jonathan paused, and again a slight smile crossed his face. "Well, at least no problems then."

"What Jonathan just said is correct," Katya interjected, nodding her head. "Russia has racial problems. We have had them here on Sakhalin. It will be an issue in the trial."

Chávez was a bit taken aback by Katya's comment. Not about race relations, but by her assumption that there would be a trial. For an instant, Chávez wondered if she already knew that there was nothing they could do to resolve the case without a trial. His appearance before the Senate Judiciary Committee was still scheduled for late March.

Chávez responded only to the race issue, "Yes, I assumed that, but we will have to get a handle on it. The problem might be different than it is in the U.S.

"Jonathan, go on. What about that night at her apartment?"

"We kissed. I liked Olga a lot. She liked me. Our relationship was forming. I thought she was beautiful, smart, interesting. If you are asking me if we had sex that night, the answer is no. By then, I knew Olga really cared for me, but I could sense that she was unsure. I guess it was because of my color. She wanted to take it one step at a time."

As Jonathan completed his answer, Chávez had two completely disparate thoughts. He already liked Jonathan; he was thoughtful, and there was even a gentle quality to him. And, it was getting cold. As to the second thought, Chávez had removed his cashmere overcoat when they entered the interview room. But now it seemed that he needed it back on. Chávez noticed Jonathan had placed his hands in his pants pockets. No wonder Jonathan was sick with a hacking cough.

Katya asked Jonathan, "Do you have a coat and gloves in your cell?"

Jonathan replied, "Yes. You know, I am in a segregation cell. Sometimes I need to put everything on to stay warm."

Katya responded, "Perhaps we can get you a heater in your cell. I will see about that myself."

Chávez made no comment but assumed Katya's statement carried with it the implication that she would pay someone to get a heater for Jonathan's cell. So be it.

Chávez put on his overcoat and continued, "Okay, Jonathan, what happened next between you and Sergova?"

"I came down to Yuzhno again in November, around Thanksgiving. There was snow here by then. We spent Saturday together, cross-country skiing out on some trails by a lake. I used a company truck to get around that weekend. I had a room at the Santa. I could tell something had changed. She was ready to commit to a relationship if I was. And I was ready."

Jonathan stopped. He was now having trouble with the words. He began again. "I've had relationships before, you know in college, and I dated a woman in Houston, where Exxon sent me right after college. But this was different. Olga's feelings for me were real, you know, honest. I felt the same about her."

Chávez broke in, "So far, you have not mentioned meeting any of Olga's friends. Are there people we can contact to prove you had a relationship with her before the night of the murder?"

Jonathan hesitated, "I don't know. I mean, I really can't recall ever speaking to someone on the street with her."

Chávez thought he knew why. Sergova was likely unsure about what her friends would think about her having a relationship with a black American man.

Chávez started again, "Okay, you saw her near the end of November. Were you intimate then?"

"No, not that night either," Jonathan replied, kind of staring past Chávez's questions.

Chávez pressed on, "So, when did you see her again?"

"It was not until my last night on Sakhalin before I went home for Christmas. There was a lot going on at the project; I pretty much worked every day until Christmas vacation."

Chávez interjected, "Did you talk during that time?"

"Yes, we talked almost every night," Jonathan reported.

"What about e-mail?" Chávez asked.

"No, we never did that. We just talked on the cell phone."

"Why not?" Chávez asked.

"I don't know. I was not in the office much. We just talked on the phone."

Chávez glanced up at Katya and said. "In America, phone records are easy to get. Sometimes the company will give them up voluntarily, but in any event, you can normally get them through a subpoena."

"It is not exactly that way here, Peter," Katya replied. "Russians don't buy phone plans like you do in America. We buy a chip that goes in the phone. When the minutes are used up, we buy more minutes that are put on the chip. Getting any records is next to impossible. There's no such thing as a private subpoena. The Russian Criminal Procedure Code requires individuals and businesses to cooperate with a government investigation. In other words, we would have to request that the Senior Investigator, Alexander Masterkov, obtain any records that might exist. If the Prokuror's office does not agree to our request, we will have to get a judge to order it."

Katya looked at Jonathan, "Do you have a Russian phone?"

"Yes, I had one. Masterkov took it when he arrested me. Olga's number is programmed into the phone," Jonathan replied.

Chávez was once again taken aback. He simply assumed that cell phone use was the same throughout the world. The records would prove the relationship. Apparently, that was not so. They would need to get a look at Jonathan's phone. Hopefully the chip would have saved all the calls back and forth.Without the records, it was going to be more difficult to establish a prior relationship between Jonathan and Sergova than he thought. Chávez brought the conversation back to Jonathan's last night with Sergova. "So what happened next?"

Jonathan again gave the impression that he wanted to choose his words carefully. Jonathan Haynes was precise—an engineer—who would suspect that he was the son of a man who had once been a drug kingpin?

"I flew down on the company plane late in the afternoon on December 20th. I stayed at the Sapporo."

"Why didn't you just plan on staying with Olga at her place?"

Hesitantly, Jonathan replied, "Well, she didn't ask me to."

"So, did you go out somewhere on the night of the 20th?"

"Yes. We decided to meet at the 777 Club. She was already there when I arrived."

"Did anything unusual happen that evening?"

Jonathan paused as if to search his memory. "No, we talked about Christmas celebrations. Olga explained how Russians recognize our Christmas on the 25th, and also celebrate their Christmas on the 7th of January. Oh, perhaps there is one thing."

Chávez injected, "What was that?" Hoping it was something helpful.

"I asked her if she was working on anything interesting."

Jonathan paused and rearranged himself in the chair. Chávez thought that it seemed to be getting even colder in the room.

"She told me that she was working on an important story, but that the story was not yet public. She seemed enthusiastic about it, but reluctant to divulge many of the details to me. It had to do with awarding contracts to Russian companies for various projects connected with the oil and gas ventures. She said she had some suspicions that some high-level officials in the region were taking bribes, making sure that certain Russian companies received the plum north/south gas pipeline contracts. She told me that she thought someone inside the administration might provide her with some corroboration. She said that she was following up. I actually think she was going to meet someone the next morning about the story, but I'm not sure."

Chávez did not react immediately to Jonathan's last comments. However, he could see the formation of a defense theory. Someone else had a motive to kill Sergova. A contract hit. The articles that he had read on the way over asserted that numerous Russian journalists had been murdered by contract killers. However, those journalists had been shot or car bombed; they had not been strangled.

Chávez said, "Did she tell you any more about the story?"

Jonathan shook his head. "No, that's all I remember."

Chávez then asked Jonathan, "What about the corruption? Do you think Olga was on to something?"

Jonathan replied, "I don't know about her specific story, but sure, there is corruption at every level of business here. It's so stupid, the Russians could have so much, but they ruin it for themselves with all their bribes and their violence."

Chávez looked over at Katya. She said nothing, her face impassive.

Chávez continued, "This might be difficult, but I need to know everything that happened at Olga's apartment. I mean *everything.*"

Jonathan paused. Again, he seemed to be getting his thoughts in order.

"This is hard to do."

Then, to see what reaction he would get, Chávez said, "Jonathan, this is not like the thing during college. It won't just go away."

Chávez studied Jonathan's face, looking for a noticeable effect from his statement about the college incident.

Jonathan seemed to register some surprise as he responded. "What happen there was stupid, but I did not rape that girl, honestly. That's why I didn't get kicked out."

Chávez glanced imperceptibly at Katya. She had a quizzical look, apparently trying to understand the importance of the exchange that had just taken place.

"Okay. Tell me what happened here." Chávez continued.

"Ah, well, we got to the apartment probably about ten p.m., something like that. Olga put on some music, traditional Russian love songs." Jonathan looked at Katya, "You know, Russians are always singing about love."

Chávez glanced at Katya, who seemed to smile self-consciously, apparently slightly embarrassed by Jonathan's comment.

"And then, uh, you know, we became affectionate."

He stopped, looking at Katya.

Katya, responding to Jonathan's glance in her direction, said, "Jonathan, I am a lawyer, just like Peter. You need to explain everything that happened that night."

Jonathan nodded to Katya and continued. "Olga told me she loved me, and we went into her bedroom. We made love. It was our first time."

"Olga told me she had not been intimate with a man for some time. We slept for a while and made love again. I finally left in a cab at about two a.m."

Chávez interjected again, "Did things get out of control?" "No." Jonathan shook his head. "Nothing like that happened. I thought we might have a future together. I tried to call her from Seattle on her cell phone, but it would just go to some kind of provider response."

Tears flooded Jonathan's eyes, and he began to cough uncontrollably. Between each cough Jonathan repeated, "I didn't kill Olga. Please believe me. I didn't kill her."

For Chávez the interview was over. He stood up and put his hand on Jonathan's shoulder.

"Jonathan, that's enough for today. We will get this figured out."

CHAPTER

10

"Yes, General. The investigative file is in order. I decided not to make Osipova review the file here. Instead, I personally copied the entire file. Ms. Osipova will obtain the copy of the file in a few minutes. Yes, General, I am satisfied we have the killer. There is nothing more to it. All of the procedures will be observed, but the trial will be a mere formality." Masterkov replied to Karpov's second phone inquiry of the day.

When he had searched Jonathan Haynes' flat in Nogliki, he found no evidence in the flat that there had been any kind of prior relationship between Haynes and Olga. There was no card from her. He had interviewed all of Haynes' co-workers. Only two, Haselton and Balmer, had heard Haynes even mention anything about a woman in Yuzhno. However, neither of them had heard anything about Olga Sergova. There was one complication, however, and that was Haynes' cell phone. Masterkov had scrolled through Haynes' phone when he had seized it. Olga's cell number was on Haynes' cell phone. Of course no one knew that he recognized the number, and Masterkov could not put that fact in his initial report without risking the possibility that his relationship with Olga would be exposed. Now, to his dismay, having checked the evidence room immediately after listening to the interview in the Detention Center, the cell phone was not there. And of course no one working in the evidence room knew anything about the disappearance of the phone. The Russian lawyers that the Prokuror's office dealt with every day would never bother to check on the evidence against their clients, so the loss of evidence that occurred periodically was never a problem. With Chávez involved it was clearly going to be a problem. The feelings that he had experienced when he had searched the Nogliki flat—feelings that someone had been there ahead of him—resurfaced. Objectively, there was nothing in the statements Haynes had made to Chávez that should have made Masterkov uncomfortable with his belief that Haynes was the murderer. Yet, some uneasiness was beginning to intrude on his thoughts. Karpov, however, could not read those thoughts. Apparently satisfied with Masterkov's answers, he hung up.

The phone rang again. Masterkov punched the intercom button. As he expected, Katya Osipova and Chávez were there for the file. Masterkov straightened his uniform, picked up the copy of the investigative file, and opened his office door.

"Ms. Osipova, how pleasant to see you." Masterkov said with a smile. He meant it. Katya Osipova was again beautifully dressed. This time her matching fur coat and hat were black, instead of the white ensemble she had worn to the airport.

"Good afternoon, Investigator. This is Peter Chávez, an American lawyer, also here on Mr. Haynes' behalf," Katya replied, gesturing toward Chávez.

Masterkov extended his hand to Chávez and addressed him with a formal greeting in Russian.

"Good afternoon, Mr. Chávez."

Chávez replied immediately, also using formal Russian. "Good afternoon, Investigator Masterkov."

For an instant longer than was polite, Masterkov stared intently at Chávez. To Masterkov's surprise, Chávez did not turn away or divert his eyes. Instead, Chávez returned his stare.

Katya broke the stare-down.

"Investigator, thank you for agreeing to give us a copy of the file. Is that the copy you have with you?"

The confrontation interrupted, Masterkov replied in Russian, "I don't understand the 'us' in your sentence, Ms. Osipova. I have the file, and you are entitled to a copy. Mr. Chávez is not a Russian lawyer. He has no authority whatsoever in this case."

"Of course, Investigator. I misspoke. You know that I am Mr. Haynes' Russian lawyer, and I am formally requesting the copy of the investigative file," Katya replied evenly.

Masterkov again looked directly at Chávez and again in Russan stated, "Mr. Chávez, I realize you have come a great distance, but there is little you can do here for Mr. Haynes. In fact, the best thing for you to do for him is get on a plane for America as soon as possible."

Chávez replied immediately in Russian, "Investigator, you could be right. Likely, I don't belong here. Ms.

Osipova is a very competent lawyer. However, my decision to stay or to go is none of your business. I intend to do as much as I am permitted to do here. I am sure you and the Prokuror General are not interested in convicting an innocent man."

Masterkov was a bit taken aback by Chávez's forceful reply. Masterkov assumed that if he mentioned Haynes' involvement in the incident at the university it had the potential to unnerve Chávez; however, it also had the potential to alert Chávez that the attorney-client privilege was not so sacrosanct in Russia. He decided to stick to the public record. "Mr. Chávez, as you will soon discover, the evidence against Mr. Haynes is overwhelming. The file will reveal that Mr. Haynes lied repeatedly to me, denying that he knew or had been with Ms. Sergova. Finally, he confessed to being with her that night."

From the corner of his eye, Masterkov saw Katya physically recoil from his assertion that Haynes had repeatedly lied about knowing or being with Olga. To his surprise, however, Chávez evidenced no outward reaction to the comment. Instead, he spoke in a calm, even tone.

"I appreciate your view of the evidence, Investigator. Often, evidence appears a certain way until it is tested and closely scrutinized. That is part of an adversarial justice system. I realize the adversarial system is something new to you."

Masterkov knew that what he was about to say should wait until he could get a look at Chávez's documents, but Chávez did not appear to intimidate easily.

Against Masterkov's better judgment, and knowing he had no capacity to carry out the threat, he could not resist one more comment. "So be it, Mr. Chávez. I should advise you that I have a number of concerns about your client and that I will now start looking at other similar murders on the island since Mr. Haynes arrived here. Perhaps Mr. Haynes is responsible for those as well."

Without waiting for a reaction, Masterkov thrust the file at Katya, stating, "In any event, Ms. Osipova, here is your copy of the investigative file."

CHAPTER

11

Chávez and Katya arrived at the courthouse in the late afternoon in the midst of a heavy snowstorm. Because Chávez had seen very few cars or buses moving about the city, he was surprised that the courthouse was a hubbub of activity. As soon as he stepped through the main door of the courthouse, his ears were assaulted by the high-pitched whine of electrical saws and the repetitive thud of large hammers, apparently tearing into plaster and wood.

At the security station Chávez and Katya were subjected to a pat-down of their outer clothing, and their briefcases were thoroughly searched. As they moved toward the interior of the building, Chávez observed a mixture of old and new. The part of the large building housing the court appeared to have two wings. The wing to the left was emitting the sounds of construction he had heard as he entered the building.

Katya, however, steered him to the right. That hallway had a bumpy linoleum floor and, similar to the Detention Center, peeling plaster walls. However, the door to the courtroom at the end of the hallway looked new, and as they opened the door they were greeted with the smell of fresh paint, wood, and new carpet. Entering the courtroom, Katya explained that this was the first courtroom that had been renovated and retrofitted to accommodate a jury trial.

Chávez scarcely heard a word, his eyes and thoughts immediately focused on the barred cage along the wall directly opposite the jury box. As Katya proudly explained the new features of the modern courtroom, Chávez could not conceive that a jury could apply the presumption of innocence required by the new Russian Constitution when the jury first viewed the defendant in a cage. Katya stopped in mid-sentence as she realized that Chávez remained fixated on the cage.

Pointing to the cage, Chávez asked, "Will Jonathan Haynes be in this cage if there is a trial?"

"Unfortunately, yes, the cage is a hold-over from our old system," Katya replied.

Chávez could see that Katya was embarrassed, and he wished that he had said nothing about the cage. In keeping with that thought, Chávez decided not to mention his other thought about the inhibiting nature of the cage. How could a lawyer communicate with a client during a trial when the client was in a cage, instead of seated at counsel table? Chávez needed to be careful about what he said to Katya. She seemed to have been somewhat unnerved by the encounter with Masterkov. Just as Masterkov had represented to them, the investigative file did contain what purported to be a statement signed by Jonathan Haynes all but confessing to killing Sergova.

Of course it all bothered Chávez. However, what concerned Chávez the most was Masterkov's comment that he "had a number of concerns" that would cause him to begin looking at other similar murders on the island. For Chávez that seemed to be a veiled mention of the university incident. Chávez had correctly predicted that Jonathan Haynes would deny committing or confessing to the murder. But how did Masterkov know about the incident? Had the border guards at the airport been able to read English and somehow discovered McCallum's report, or had Masterkov somehow searched his briefcase or his room? Or was the jail bugged?

Chávez immediately pushed those thoughts aside as the courtroom door opened and Masterkov entered. As Masterkov, dressed in his crisply pressed blue military-style uniform, passed by them, he nodded but said nothing. An instant later, the bailiffs entered from a side door, escorting Jonathan Haynes into the cage. Jonathan's hands and feet were restricted by separate chain arrangements wrapped about his body. To Chávez's surprise, the guards motioned him over to the cage.

Jonathan Haynes looked up at Chávez, his face ashen, just as it had been the evening before when Chávez had confronted him about his initial lies to Masterkov claiming that he did not know Olga Sergova. And, just as he had done in the Detention Center, Jonathan kept repeating, "Please believe me, Mr. Chávez, I did not kill Olga. I loved her."

Chávez held his finger to his closed mouth and turned away watching the Prokuror's deputy enter the courtroom.

Chávez's dislike of Andrey Barbatov was instant and visceral. Barbatov, also dressed in a blue military-style uniform, appeared to be slightly less than six feet tall. His dark hair was plastered to his head, set in position by an abundance of oil. Barbatov acknowledged Katya as he made his way to the counsel table. Chávez wondered if the sneer that Barbatov directed at him was temporary or a permanent fixture of the large, flat, and slightly pock-marked face. Barbatov's appearance suggested to Chávez that Barbatov could have played a character in *The Addams Family*.

After receiving the investigative file from Masterkov, Katya and Chávez had had only the evening to prepare for the morning's hearing. Katya had estimated the chances of a favorable ruling permitting Chávez to repre-sent Jonathan in the court proceedings as slim to none. Chávez felt ashamed to even think it, but a ruling pro-hibiting him from representing Jonathan Haynes in court could work out just right. He could believe he had done what he could to satisfy his debt to Michael Haynes and get on the first plane home. Chávez took his seat in the first row directly across from Masterkov, who stared straight ahead.

Chief Judge of the Sakhalin region, Aleksey Pavlovich Vasilyuk, entered the courtroom from a side door. Judge Vasilyuk was in his middle forties, slightly built with a thin hawk-like face. According to Katya, Vasi-lyuk was a former prosecutor, smart and ambitious. In spite of the new adversarial system mandated by the Russian Constitution, Judge Vasilyuk had never acquitted a criminal defendant. Katya suspected that Vasilyuk's ambition kept him keenly aware of the Kremlin's attitude toward Russian justice.

Katya had based her motion to permit Chávez to represent Jonathan in the court proceedings on an obscure provision of the new Russian Criminal Procedure Code, permitting a criminal defendant to designate a relative or a friend as their representative in court proceedings. Katya confirmed Chávez's initial observation that the provision did not seem at all relevant to Jonathan's case. Instead, it likely was intended for use in the very rural areas of Siberia where there were no lawyers.

That was where Judge Vasilyuk began.

"Ms. Osipova, your client already has a lawyer; that is you. How can Article 49 of the Criminal Procedure Code apply?"

"Your Honor, I can represent to the court that it is Mr. Haynes' desire to have Mr. Chávez, not me, represent him and speak for him, should Your Honor grant this important motion," Katya responded, gesturing toward the cage and the slumped, chained body of Jonathan Haynes.

"Well, Mr. Barbatov, what is wrong with that? The defendant is American. Why not let an American lawyer defend him?"

Barbatov's face quickly turned crimson. He seemed shocked that Judge Vasilyuk would even consider the question.

"Your Honor, it's preposterous, an American lawyer in a Russian courtroom. As you said, Article 49 is not relevant here. The city has plenty of lawyers. And Ms.

Osipova, a former prosecutor in Vladivostok, is perfectly capable of representing Mr. Haynes. Your Honor, it's unthinkable."

Chávez quickly stole a glance in Masterkov's direction. There was nothing. Masterkov stared straight ahead, his face blank.

Barbatov continued his diatribe against Chávez and the American criminal defense bar.

"Your Honor, you know that the American legal system is corrupt, dominated by American corporations on one side, and the sly, fast-talking trial lawyers on the other. Mr. Chávez comes from the worst of that group, American criminal defense lawyers. They will stop at nothing to pervert justice on behalf of their murdering, child raping clients."

Judge Vasilyuk allowed Barbatov to rail against the ruthless, underhanded, unethical American criminal defense lawyers until it appeared that Barbatov had run out of epithets. As Barbatov paused, Judge Vasilyuk interjected.

"That is all very well, Mr. Barbatov. I understand your point. Do you have information specific to Mr. Chávez? Has Mr. Chávez ever been in trouble in America? Has he committed any crimes there?"

"I don't know, Your Honor, and I don't see how it matters," Barbatov shot back.

"Well, I do, Mr. Barbatov. I checked with the Oregon State Bar Association. Their records are on the Web and open to anyone. Mr. Chávez has committed no crimes, no ethical violations. According to a service called Martindale something or other, he enjoys the highest ratings for both skill and ethical behavior. You certainly know that he has been nominated by the American president to a federal judgeship in Oregon, the state he comes from."

Chávez pondered how small the Internet had made the world. But where was Judge Vasilyuk going? How could he justify a favorable ruling under Article 49? The answer was quick and stunning.

"Mr. Barbatov and Ms. Osipova, are you aware of the Mutual Cooperation Agreement finally negotiated yesterday in Moscow between the president of the American Bar Association and the president of the new Union of Russian Lawyers?"

Barbatov and Katya both shook their heads no.

"I received a copy of the agreement by fax this morning. There is a provision in the agreement stating that Russian lawyers and American lawyers should be permitted to engage in the practice of law on a very limited basis in each country. The details for temporary admission in each country are being drafted."

Barbatov, apparently unable to contain himself, jumped to his feet, interrupting, "Your Honor, that's not law, that's just some big-shot lawyers patting each other on the back. It does not apply to us."

"Sit down, Mr. Barbatov. I am not through yet. Mr. Chávez, please approach the bench." Chávez rose and slowly made his way to the bench, trying to anticipate what would occur next. Judge Vasilyuk shook his head slightly as if to expose his own misgivings about what was about to happen.

"Sir, I am going to grant the motion," Judge Vasilyuk said firmly. "You will be permitted to represent Mr.

Haynes on this side of the bar. I understand that you speak Russian. I hope that you are fluent because you will not have a private interpreter in the courtroom. Ms. Osipova, you will be co-counsel. Mr. Haynes will have an independent court interpreter. Trial will begin on March 1st.

"Let me say this, Mr. Chávez. Think hard about what you are doing. You don't know Russian criminal procedure—you don't know Russian ways. Your presence in the courtroom could guarantee that Mr. Haynes never leaves a Russian prison."

CHAPTER

12

U nlike Barbatov, who rushed from the courtroom, Masterkov moved at normal pace not wanting to reveal any of the outright shock he was experiencing from Judge Vasilyuk's ruling. Moments after Masterkov had returned to his office, Karpov called on the intercom summoning him to Karpov's office. Masterkov, Barbatov, and Karpov were now seated around the conference table in Karpov's spacious office.

Without appearing to be too intent, Masterkov listened closely to the exchange between Karpov and Barbatov.

"General, you must appeal this ruling immediately; there is no basis in law," Barbatov pleaded.

"What about the Mutual Cooperation Agreement with the American Bar Association the judge relied on? That is some basis for the ruling," Karpov replied, gesturing to the fax copy of the agreement arrayed in front of him.

Barbatov retorted, "Regardless of what these lawyers think they are doing, the Duma would need to pass a law permitting foreign lawyers to appear in court. Make the

Supreme Court order it. Besides, it will delay the trial a year. We can't be ready for a jury trial in two weeks. It's just not right. Investigator Masterkov will know even more about Haynes by then. I sense Ms. Osipova and Mr. Chávez want a quick trial. Don't give in to the American lawyer."

Karpov did not answer immediately. He looked out the window for a few seconds, and then he got up and refilled his cup with tea from the samovar.

"Andrey, you have made some excellent points. It's more complicated than you realize. My decision is final; there will be no appeal of this ruling. Besides, you will have an even greater advantage over an American lawyer unfamiliar with our system."

Masterkov studied Karpov's face closely. He concluded that Karpov's pained expression as he phrased his decision revealed some kind of inner conflict. It appeared someone else was calling the shots.

Masterkov had shut off his computer and left for his apartment as soon as the meeting had ended. He now sat in the living room of his flat, sipping cognac and replaying the day's events over and over in his head.

Why did Vasilyuk make such an unprecedented ruling? Why had Karpov accepted the judge's ruling? They had a right to appeal the ruling to Moscow and keep Haynes locked up for a year, maybe eighteen months, without a trial. He would have that much more time to try to link Haynes to the murders of two other Sakhalin women that fit within the time Haynes had been on the island, something he had no time for with the quick trial date that Vasilyuk had set.

There was only one answer: the Kremlin was involved and pulling the strings. The Kremlin had interfered with judicial proceedings at other times when it deemed it necessary. They had used the courts to confiscate the assets of Yukos Oil and to imprison Khodorkovsky—so much for the new constitutional requirement that the branches of government be co-equal and separate. Apparently, as the Kremlin saw it, this would be a show trial, the new Russian adversarial system providing justice for all the world to see—and doing it quickly. Perhaps it was another way to demonstrate that Russia again was a player in the international community. The Kremlin's control over every branch of government and every aspect of Russian life was complete. But would this be the show trial that the Kremlin wanted or had in mind? It struck Masterkov as a reckless decision and one that everyone involved might regret.

One last thought lingered as Masterkov again listened to his secret recording of Chávez's initial interview with Haynes at the Detention Center. Haynes had told Chávez that Olga Sergova was working on a major corruption story involving the regional administration. Likely it was the same story that Olga's research assistant, Natalia Kurilova, had hinted at in his initial interview with her. He picked up his cell phone and replayed Olga's message. She had to have been referring to the same investigation. His intuition told him that Chávez might be capable of somehow using that fact to screw up the whole thing.

CHAPTER
13

It was dark when Chávez and Katya left the courthouse and walked through a light snow toward Katya's office. A few blocks from the courthouse Katya suggested they stop for dinner in a nearby restaurant.

Unlike the crumbling faded countenance of the outside of the building, the inside was inviting. The dining room was softly lit. A circular fireplace in the middle of the room emitted a warm glow. They were seated at a table near a window. Snowflakes floated through the window light and then disappeared into the darkness. Chávez ordered a bottle of champagne. The ruling had put Katya in a state of euphoria, although she was certain that Karpov would appeal the ruling. Chávez thought differently. His instinctive wariness told him that the case was quickly becoming about a lot more than a murder in a remote part of the Russian Far East. At any rate, he hid his disappointment at not having an immediate ticket out of the Russian Far East and the fact there was no readily apparent defense. The prosecution had means, motive, and opportunity—the classic elements of a "lock and load" murder case, as the American prosecutors referred to open-and-shut cases. Even if Haynes' initial lies were somehow excluded, it was Haynes' hair, Haynes' semen, and Haynes' fingerprint. Jonathan Haynes had admitted to everything but putting his hands around Sergova's neck. To Chávez, it seemed that he too was now imprisoned in Russia and being marched to his own professional execution. What a fucked up mess.

Chávez eventually turned his thoughts away from his impending doom to the beautiful woman seated across from him. It had been a long time since he had been single and interested. He had slept with two different women since Claire's death. Each woman had been attractive and pleasant, and each had a firm body and good mechanics. But that was just what each experience had been—mechanics. There was no intimacy. Chávez started the conversation cautiously.

"Katya, is your husband a lawyer or somehow involved in the legal profession?"

"Peter, I am not married. How did you get the idea that I was married?" Katya answered quickly, her eyebrows arched in surprise. Chávez had doubted that she was married but had asked the question just to confirm his belief.

He responded to Katya, "I just assumed that a beautiful and intelligent woman like you was married."

Katya smiled, but the smile faded quickly as she continued, "I was married. My husband's name was Konstantin."

Although Katya was not finished, Chávez, to his own complete surprise, interrupted her. "I seem to have upset you, I'm sorry, I didn't mean to. I seem to do that frequently."

Katya's smile returned immediately, "No, no, I'm not upset by your question, it's just that what happened is sometimes hard for me to talk about."

"I interrupted. Go ahead, please." Chávez said.

"I am not from Sakhalin. I was born in Rostov-on-the-Don. Are you familiar with the city of Rostov?" Katya asked.

"No."

"Rostov is a large city in southern Russia on the Don River. It is very beautiful there. Rostov is considered the gateway city to the Caucasus, the last large city before you enter that region."

"You mean it is on the way to Chechnya?" Chávez asked.

"Yes, unfortunately that is how it is viewed today," Katya answered.

"How long did you live in Rostov?"

"My father was an officer in the army. He became a general when I was fifteen, and we then moved to Moscow."

Chávez was fascinated—the daughter of a Soviet general. "Are your parents still living?" he asked.

"Yes, my father is retired from the army and now sells agricultural equipment. He and my mother still live in Moscow. I also have a younger sister who also lives in Moscow."

Katya paused, so Chávez asked, "Before you got your Marshall scholarship, had you ever been out of the Soviet Union?"

"Yes, actually, when I was sixteen I went to New York. My father briefly assisted with a matter at the United Nations."

"What did you think when you first saw the United States?" Chávez asked.

Katya furrowed her brow as if reliving some previous unpleasant event. "Funny you should ask, Peter. Two days after my parents and I arrived in New York, I asked my father if it was all a big lie."

"What do you mean, a big lie?" Chávez responded.

"I asked my father if everything we had been taught about Russia being the greatest country in the world was a lie. It seemed obvious to me that America was far more advanced and far greater."

"How did your father answer you?"

"He told me never to ask that question again and in particular to never mention anything like that in public."

Chávez was unsure how to respond, so he said nothing. Instead he focused on Katya's perfect skin and sparkling eyes. Katya took another sip of her champagne and returned to the more recent events in her life.

"Konstantin was a submarine officer. We were living in Vladivostok, which then was the headquarters for the Pacific Naval Fleet when our country, you know, the Soviet Union, fell apart in 1991. Within a year, Konstantin was forced from the Navy."

"What did your husband do after that?" Chávez asked.

"He got into the fishing industry." Katya paused, and then she seemed to force the next words from her mouth. "Konstantin was murdered four years ago. He and his partner were doing well, and they were getting business that previously had gone to other companies in Vladivostok and just north in Nakhodka. Enemies were made. I am sure you have heard of the Russian Mafia. My husband and his partner were murdered. The Vladivostok Prokuror has never charged anyone."

Katya paused, then she added, "Peter, Russia, particularly the Russian Far East, can be a very dangerous place. You have to be very careful here."

They both grew quiet as Chávez contemplated the danger and the corruption that could easily become a part of the case in which he was now involved. Eventually, the conversation returned to more pleasant topics as Katya asked Chávez a number of questions about his life and his career. As they enjoyed an after-dinner cognac, the saxophone player began a soft jazzy number. The couple in the booth next to them got up and walked to a small dance floor where they began to dance. At that moment Chávez desperately wanted to hold the beautiful Russian woman seated across from him. More than that, he wanted to feel her body pressing against his. Chávez knew it would be awkward if she declined his invitation to dance, but hell, everything else was a mess, why not give it a try?

"Katya, would you like to dance?" Chávez said as he began to get out of his chair.

Although he and Katya had been speaking in English all evening, Katya answered with a common Russian phrase, "*Da, konechno,*" ("Yes, of course") and took Chávez's outstretched hand. At the small dance floor he enfolded her in his arms, pulling her close. Immediatedly, he sensed the stunning curvature of her body and the swell of her breasts, experiencing a feeling of pleasure too long absent from his life. Unfortunately, the saxphone player's set ended with that song.

They walked in a light snow to Katya's office where they picked up her car. As Chávez was getting out of the car at the Sapporo, Katya reached a hand toward him. He reached back and squeezed her hand. Their eyes met as he said good night.

About a half hour after he had returned to his hotel room, his thoughts alternating between how to deal with Jonathan's initial lies to Masterkov and his growing attraction to Katya, his cell phone rang. Chávez picked up his phone hoping it was Katya intending in some way to prolong their evening together. To his delight, it was Katya; however, her voice was all business.

"Peter, when I returned to my flat there was a message on my phone. It was from a man named Ivan Dudinov, and he says he has some information for us. Our firm has done some business with Ivan, and he has proved reliable in the past."

"Did he say what information he had?" Chávez asked.

"No, Peter, only that it was important and that he wanted to meet. I will call and arrange for us to meet with him as soon as possible. I just wanted to let you know right away," Katya continued in a serious voice.

Chávez replied. "Thanks, Katya, for letting me know. Your call gives me some confidence. I was just about to e-mail each of my senators to update them on my situation here. I told them I would be here only briefly, perhaps as little as a few days. Now, thanks to your excellent lawyering, I will be here awhile—unless Karpov appeals, and my gut says that he won't. The international press will soon start to focus on my presence here in Russia. As I said at dinner, I think you are a wonderful lawyer."

Katya responded, not mentioning anything about his impending judgeship. "Thank you, Peter, your confidence means a lot to me. I will talk to you in the morning. Good night."

Images of Katya and Claire seeming to be the same person plagued Chávez as he finally drifted off to a troubled sleep.

CHAPTER

14

The cell phone number that Natalia Kurilova had given Masterkov during his initial interview with her was no longer active. Kurilova's neighbors at her apartment building uniformly stated that they had not seen her for at least two weeks. The editor of *Sovietsky Sakhalin* tried not to appear hostile. However, he would tell Masterkov only that she had quit her job and no longer worked for the newspaper.

Masterkov had waited a day for the latest blizzard to clear and then headed north for the village of Tymovskoye located in the approximate middle of the island. He was now on a narrow snow-drifted road outside Tymovskoye. He was looking for a cabin that the local game warden had informed him was Kurilova's parents' residence.

The outskirts of Tymovskoye looked like a place time had forgotten. The wires on utility poles were ragged or missing altogether. Masterkov guessed that because of the repeated metal wire thefts by the local inhabitants, attempts at rural electrification had long since been abandoned. Checking his distance from the village center,

Masterkov began looking intently out the right side of his Pathfinder for a cabin set far back from the road.

Just as he reached the ten-kilometer mark, he caught a glimpse of a small snow-covered cabin nearly hidden by large trees. Because of the snow depth there was no vehicle access to the small abode. Masterkov shut the engine off, deciding to leave the Pathfinder in the ruts in the snow that he had driven in for the last ten kilometers. Before getting out of the car, Masterkov removed his shoulder holster containing the Stechkin automatic that he had carried since the early days of his career in Moscow. He placed the shoulder holster and weapon under the driver's seat. According to the game warden, Kurilova's father was one of the most well known hunters and suspected poachers in the region. Masterkov concluded that if Natalia Kurilova was in hiding with her parents as he suspected, his chances of getting her to talk to him were increased if he was not armed. Still, it left him vulnerable to her father and other unforeseen events. That vulnerability was not complete, however. A tiny MSP pistol was hidden inside his right fur-lined boot.

Masterkov had walked for a couple of minutes in the deep snow when he first saw the shadowy figure in the trees to his left. He was a short distance from the house when the man came into full view, a hunting rifle raised to his shoulder. In response, Masterkov raised his arms and shouted, "I am Alexander Sergeevich Masterkov. I am not armed."

Masterkov estimated that the man with the rifle still raised and moving steadily closer looked to be in his late forties or early fifties, but trim and in good physical condition. He was wearing hunters' camouflage and he had a bushy red beard, seemingly uncut for some time.

Before Masterkov could say more, the man barked, "What do you want here?"

Masterkov did not answer the inquiry directly. Instead he replied, "Are you Mikhail Viktorovich Kurilov?"

The man shot back, "I am asking the questions. What do you want here?"

Masterkov decided to answer directly. "I am Senior Investigator Alexander Sergeevich Masterkov. I want to speak briefly with Natalia Kurilova. I believe you may be her father. I told you that I am unarmed. I mean you and your daughter no harm. Please feel free to search me. I do not have a weapon."

Keeping the rifle raised, his finger on the trigger, the man replied, "Turn around and walk back to your car. You are in the wrong place. Turn around and retrace your steps out. If you look back, it will be the last movement you make."

Masterkov turned in the direction of the car, but as he did, he repeated, "I am unarmed. It would be much better for your daughter to talk with me here. I don't understand why she left Yuzhno."

The man said nothing in reply. Instead, he jammed the rifle barrel into Masterkov's back as if to keep him moving toward the road and his car.

Almost the instant the rifle barrel hit his back Masterkov heard a young woman's voice, "Papa, stop."

CHAPTER

15

Chávez could sense Katya's anxiety as he helped her from the taxi over the dirty rutted snow toward the entrance to the Grey Kat Bar located in the seedy Yinitar section of Yuzhno. Inside, the bar reeked of cigarette smoke and vodka. Every man in the bar turned and stared at Katya as they made their way to a small booth toward the back of the bar. Chávez surmised that the overpowering smell of vodka in the bar emanated, not just from the open bottles and overflowing shot glasses, but also from the men's pores.

Seconds seemed like hours to Chávez as he watched Katya turn her beautiful head each time they heard the door open.

"Katya, are you sure this is the bar that this Dudinov mentioned?" Chávez asked, trying not to reveal his own growing concern with their surroundings.

"Yes, Peter, I have been here before. This is the bar." Katya replied, looking over toward the front door.

Incredulous, Chávez inquired in a low voice, "You've actually been here by yourself?"

Although Katya initially chuckled at the question, Chávez could still sense the stress in her voice and the movement of her hands.

"No, not by myself, but I came here with Dudinov once."

"What did you mean in the cab when you said Dudinov's methods were a bit different?" Chávez continued, hoping Katya's answer to this question would assure him that Dudinov was an investigator of sorts and not Katya's current or former lover.

Just then the door opened and Chávez observed a tall man, about six foot two, with close cropped gray hair sitting over a weathered but handsome face, step into the bar. He was clad in an expensive fur-lined, three-quarter-length leather coat. Chávez thought it odd that not a single one of the bar patrons even glanced at the new arrival heading directly to Chávez and Katya's booth.

Katya greeted the man in Russian. In turn, the man reached out and, in the Russian tradition, kissed Katya on both cheeks. The man then turned to Chávez and extended his hand, announcing in Russian, "I am Dudinov, Ivan Ivanovich."

Dudinov's grip was strong, consistent with his well-muscled frame. Chávez returned the introduction in Russian, sensing that English would not be used in the conversation.

Katya began the discussion. "Ivan, I told Mr. Chávez that you had some information that might be of help to our client."

Before speaking Dudinov took a sip from the bottle of Baltica beer that had arrived at the table, though Chávez had not observed Dudinov make any sign that he wanted a beer, much less the brand.

"Okay. Let's get down to business. I have some information for you. And, I think there may be more out there that can help your client," Dudinov said looking directly at Chávez.

"Sounds good," Chávez said, glancing around the bar to see if any of the patrons were overly interested in what was transpiring with Dudinov. Vodka seemed their only concern.

Dudinov began. "Not long after Sergova's murder was reported on TV, I happened to be in the bar at the Eurasia Hotel. I know the woman who manages the girls there. She sat with me at the bar for a few minutes. While we shared a drink she asked me if I had heard about the murder of the journalist Sergova. When I said I had seen a report on TV and had read about it in the paper, she said one of her girls had told her an interesting story. By the way, there should be little doubt that Sergova had made any number of enemies."

As Dudinov paused for a sip of Baltica, Chávez commented. "So we are talking about a brothel, and something that a madam told you she had picked up from one of the prostitutes."

Dudinov nodded nonchalantly, and said, "Sure. They cater mostly to Asian men."

Chávez nodded, signaling for Dudinov to continue with the story.

"She said that sometime in December, one of her girls told her about an event that occurred with one of her customers. As the guy was getting undressed, an envelope fell out of his coat pocket. He did not seem to notice it. When he went to the toilet, the girl—Tatiana's her name—picked up the things that fell out and put them back into his coat.

"Two days later, she saw a story about the Sergova woman in the paper and recognized her picture. That is when she came to my friend. She told her that one of the items that she had picked up was an envelope, and in the envelope was a photo. She thought that the woman in the photo was very attractive and that she had seen a photo of the woman before. She took the photo out of the envelope for a closer look. When she did, she noticed that something was written on the back of the picture, she thought a Yuzhno address."

Dudinov then paused for another swig of his Baltica. During the pause Chávez asked, "There is more, I hope. Was the guy Asian?"

Dudinov smiled and said, "Yes, a bit more. Tatiana told the woman that the customer was a Georgian."

"How did she know he was a Georgian?" Chávez asked. "I have to confess I don't know enough about Russia to understand the significance."

Again a slight smile appeared on Dudinov's face. "Stalin was a Georgian. In Russia, Georgians seemed to have captured the market for hired killers."

The image of the proverbial hit man from Detroit almost caused Chávez to smile.

"When Tatiana put the envelope back in the customer's coat, she also felt what she was sure was a gun."

Chávez immediately interjected, "Can we get to this Tatiana to talk with her as soon as possible? What is her last name? I would like to speak to her personally."

Dudinov responded matter of factly, "She is gone."

"What do you mean she is gone?" Chávez asked.

"Russian women like Tatiana are much sought after in Southeast Asia. I did a little checking before I came here to meet you. She is somewhere in Thailand or Vietnam—either by her own choice or otherwise."

Immediately Chávez asked, "Can she be found there fairly quickly?"

Dudinov never answered directly. Instead, he began an inquiry of his own. "Mr. Chávez, I have read about your case in the paper, and I saw your arrival to the island on television. Do you really think your involvement here is the best thing for your client?"

Inwardly, Chávez fumed at the question. Judge Vasilyuk, then Masterkov, and now this guy questioning Chávez's involvement in the case. Who the hell did this guy think he was? Outwardly, Chávez remained impassive and replied in a measured cadence.

"Thank you, it's a legitimate question. There is a history between my client's father and myself. So this is the way it is, regardless of what people think about my presence here. I will be representing Jonathan Haynes in court unless the Prokuror changes his mind and appeals the judge's ruling to Moscow."

Dudinov smiled a bit, which Chávez inferred was a mixture of incredulousness and, he hoped, respect at the straight answer that he had just received to his question.

"Mr. Chávez, I know a thing or two about you. You have over five hundred entries on Google. I know you are a Vietnam veteran. I know that Jonathan Haynes' father saved your life in Vietnam thirty-some years ago. I also know that you are considered a very good lawyer in your little corner of the world. But this is Russia. Bluntly, you have no chance of succeeding here without my help. You have no idea what you are up against. If it wishes, the Kremlin can control everything, including the so-called justice system. Right now, both Karpov and Judge Vasilyuk could be getting their orders from the Kremlin or, even worse for you and your client, from the very people that had Sergova killed, assuming your client is not the killer. And then there is always Masterkov. You have no idea how dangerous that man is. I would not be surprised to find out that he is former KGB. You were in Vietnam, right? I recall reading about a snake there, a bamboo viper. I think they called it a "step and a half"—you are dead within a step and a half after the bite. That's just how deadly Masterkov is. The good thing is that Masterkov and Karpov seem rarely to be in perfect accord. Karpov always has some other angle—always good for Karpov."

Chávez concluded that Dudinov was thorough if nothing else. Chávez then turned the conversation back to Dudinov. "Mr. Dudinov, Katya told me that you were at one time an officer in the Russian Special Forces and that you served in Afghanistan and Chechnya. She told me that on occasion her firm has retained you to find people that did not want to be found or property that debtors were hiding." Again Chávez asked, "Could you find this Tatiana?"

A slight smile crossed Ivan's lips. "You mean you want to hire me, like you would a private investigator in

America. Like that American actor, Tom Selleck, in *Magnum P.I?"*

Chávez could not help but smile back. "Sure, except the real-life work of investigators in America is hardly what you have seen in American movies or on television. Mr. Dudinov, I have to assume that you are smart and capable. But what I need from you, if we can work this out, is your loyalty. In America we have confidentiality rules to which lawyers and their investigators adhere. I realize that this is not such a well-known or accepted principle here. But I will need loyalty and confidentiality from you."

There was no hesitation in Dudinov's response. "You can dispense with your lectures about confidentiality and loyalty. For me, this will be a business deal. You pay me, and I will see if there is anything out there that might help your client. It's as simple as that."

Chávez knew, however, that he really had no choice in the matter, even though he knew so little about Dudinov. Dudinov likely had contacts on Sakhalin, and in the Russian Far East for that matter, that he could never access. He needed Dudinov, though he had no real idea whether Dudinov could do the job, or whether he would just take the money and claim that the only evidence he could find pointed to Jonathan Haynes as the murderer.

Chávez replied, "OK, let's get down to it. Tell me what you will do for us and how much it will cost."

CHAPTER

16

Masterkov sat down in a back row of spectator benches in the courtroom. The hearing on Chávez's motion to suppress Haynes' custodial statements was scheduled for two-thirty in the afternoon. Chávez had filed the motion three days after Vasilyuk's ruling permitting Chávez to appear in court. Masterkov was impressed. Almost from the moment that Judge Vasilyuk ruled that Chávez could appear in court as Haynes' lawyer, Chávez had started to use the new criminal procedure code. Masterkov had always believed that the Russian Constitution and the new Russian Criminal Procedure Code allowed for motions to suppress and to exclude evidence from trial like the one that Chávez had filed. However, no defense lawyer on Sakhalin had ever filed such a motion. Criminal cases on Sakhalin still proceeded much as they had done in Soviet times—a paper trial mostly. The Prokuror's deputy would read in court the pertinent reports in the investigative file, and, at the defense lawyer's prompting, the defendant would confess in court and ask for leniency.

Despite Barbatov's assurance that he would not be called as a witness during the hearing, Masterkov thought otherwise and had taken the time to review his reports. Barbatov still did not get it. The Kremlin had to be involved, likely controlling both Judge Vasilyuk and the Prokuror's office. Masterkov hoped that was what accounted for Karpov's excessive interest in the case. The Kremlin would show the American president and the world that the Russian Constitution and the Russian judicial system were every bit America's equal. Masterkov thought it was a risky move. Things, evidence, and witnesses disappeared in Russia. Chávez had already made a written demand to have Haynes' cell phone independently examined. At some point Masterkov would have to answer the demand. Although Kurilova had told Masterkov at her parents cabin that she knew nothing more than she had told him in the patrol car, Masterkov's gut told him there was more, and not knowing what the "more" was gnawed at him.

Masterkov glanced at Haynes' signed statement admitting that he had initially lied about even knowing Olga, then admitting he had had dinner with her, then admitting that he had been in her apartment, and then finally admitting he had had sexual intercourse with her. In extracting the statements from Haynes, Masterkov had used many of the interrogation techniques he had learned as a young man in the Moscow Homicide Unit—periods of isolation, photographs of prisoners in freezing cold prisons, no sleep, and finally a friendly gesture. None of those details were contained in the official reports in the investigative file. Despite Karpov's directive early on in the case to confine the investigation solely to Haynes, and despite his desire to bring Olga Sergova's killer to justice, he would not lie. It would be up to Chávez, however, to discover all of the details of Haynes' custodial statements.

Masterkov had been so absorbed in his thoughts that he had not noticed that Chávez and Katya had entered the courtroom and were huddled in conversation at counsel table. It was clear to Masterkov that there was a relationship beyond the defense of Jonathan Haynes developing between Chávez and Katya Osipova. Barbatov was in his Deputy Prokuror's blue uniform, staring into space. As usual, Barbatov's black hair seemed to gleam from too much oil.

As the clerk banged the gavel, Masterkov closed his file and watched Judge Vasilyuk enter the courtroom, his black robe catching air and flying out behind him. After glancing about the courtroom, apparently making sure all the participants were there, including an even thinner Jonathan Haynes slumped in the cage, Judge Vasilyuk called the case.

"Mr. Barbatov, Mr. Chávez, and Ms. Osipova have filed with me a document entitled 'Motion to Exclude Alleged Incriminating Statement.' Mr. Barbatov, do you have a copy of the document, and are you prepared for the hearing today?"

Just as Masterkov thought he would, Barbatov sprang from his chair and in a loud voice, almost shouting, replied, "Your Honor, these tactics are an outrage. Apparently, Mr. Chávez can't read Russian or refuses to read our rules. There is nothing the defense can do here. The statement signed by the defendant Haynes is an official document already in the investigative file. It can't be removed. Senior Investigator Masterkov has officially attested that defendant Haynes signed the confession and that he did so voluntarily. There is nothing to discuss. The court should deny the motion now."

To Masterkov's amazement, Barbatov then wheeled around on one heel and returned to his seat at the counsel table, apparently satisfied he had done all that was needed. Masterkov could not help the bemusement he was experiencing. There seemed to be a disconnect between Karpov's decision not to appeal the ruling permitting Chávez to appear in court and Barbatov's conduct trying to protect the old ways. Why not a disconnect? After all, this was Russia.

Masterkov glanced down at the statement one more time. He doubted Barbatov had done all that he needed to do to defeat Chávez's claim. To the contrary, Masterkov was sure he would, at some point, play a role in the proceeding.

CHAPTER

17

The instant Barbatov turned and headed back to his chair at counsel table Chávez stood and walked briskly to the podium. Obviously, Barbatov favored the old Soviet inquisitorial system in which the Prokuror made the rules, had all the power, and the judge and the defense attorney were mere scenery. It was clear to Chávez that Barbatov had no intention of conforming to the procedure that the new Russian Constitution and Criminal Procedure Code authorized, giving judges the power to exclude evidence from a trial when governmental agents violated a provision of the Constitution or the Criminal Procedure Code. Barbatov would not voluntarily permit Chávez to question Masterkov in the courtroom. Chávez had to find a way to make Masterkov a witness. He suspected that the decision to permit him to defend Haynes in court, which still had not been appealed, came directly from the Kremlin, and he needed to take full advantage of the window of opportunity that had been opened for him.

"Your Honor," Chávez began, "Mr. Barbatov apparently wishes that Article 51 of the Russian Constitution and Article 46 and 47 of the new Procedure Code did not exist. Under those articles Mr. Haynes had a constitutional right to have the American Consulate in Vladivostok contacted before he was questioned, and he had a right to be advised of his right to a lawyer before answering any questions. Nothing in the reports Investigator Masterkov has placed in the official investigation file show that those procedures were followed. The Russian Constitution and the new Criminal Procedure Code demand that those rights be observed. Instead of denying our motion, you should grant the motion, Your Honor."

Judge Vasilyuk did not wait for Barbatov to mount a rebuttal. Instead, he responded directly to Chávez. "Mr. Chávez, Investigator Masterkov's report regarding your client's statement says, and I quote, 'All of the investigation in this case was done in accordance with the Russian Constitution and the Russian Code of Criminal Procedure.' Why isn't that sufficient for me to reject your assertions regarding your client's rights?"

Barbatov immediately jumped up and exclaimed, "Precisely, your Honor. Nothing more should be required."

At that moment, Chávez understood how it would be in this Russian courtroom—in some respects not so much different than some American courtrooms. The judge would create the appearance that both sides were equal. However, throughout the case the judge would assist the prosecution in various ways, by excusing mistakes, suggesting legal arguments not presented by the Prokuror, and sometimes belittling or showing undeserved irritation with the defense lawyer in front of the jury.

Chávez had concluded, however, that he had an ally in the courtroom that he could use to counter Judge Vasilyuk's subtle and not so subtle efforts to thwart his attempts to assert Jonathan Haynes' rights under the Russian Constitution. Since the international press began arriving in great numbers, Katya's office had provided the press with a steady stream of information explaining how the Russian Constitution and the new Criminal Procedure Code protected the rights of criminal defendants and permitted a jury trial.

Chávez turned and looked in the direction of the press assembled in the courtroom. From the corner of his left eye he saw Judge Vasilyuk's head also swivel in that direction. Then he answered the judge's argument. "Your Honor, I appreciate your point. The problem, however, is that Investigator Masterkov is not the judge. You are. As I understand it, the system is different now."

Chávez hoped that the veiled reference to the old days when the Prokurors and investigators had all the power would hit hard on Judge Vasilyuk. "Investigator Masterkov's conclusion that he did everything according to the Constitution is irrelevant. The power to make that conclusion resides only with you, Your Honor. And the only way that you can fairly decide that is for Investigator Masterkov to explain each of his actions to you from the moment he took Mr. Haynes into custody at the airport." Chávez then turned in Masterkov's direction. "I call Investigator Masterkov as a witness."

Barbatov was on his feet again. "No, Your Honor, he has no right to present witnesses. You know it is not proper."

Chávez had seen the look before, usually on the face of a witness realizing that he or she had walked into a trap that was about to shut. Only this time it was on Judge Vasilyuk's face.

"Mr. Barbatov, I see that Investigator Masterkov is here. I believe it advisable that you call him as a witness."

"Your Honor, this is highly irregular, I ..."

Judge Vasilyuk's interruption was thunderous. "Enough, Mr. Barbatov. Either you question Masterkov, or I will permit Mr. Chávez to do so."

Barbatov shook his head one last time then uttered the words Chávez had hoped to hear. "Investigator Masterkov, please come forward."

Chávez knew, however, that the victory could still be a Pyrrhic one. Judge Vasilyuk controlled everything. Chávez watched Masterkov, his face completely impassive, rise and stride toward Judge Vasilyuk, who advised him of the penalty for perjury. Masterkov signed a written perjury warning, then walked to the witness box where he stood behind a podium, waiting for the first question.

Chávez wondered which made a witness more uncomfortable, sitting in a chair when questioned, as was the American tradition, or standing, as Chávez had just learned was the Russian tradition. In any event, Chávez took a moment to observe Masterkov standing erect at the podium, apparently unfazed by the legal wrangling, projecting an air of confidence. Chávez was sure Masterkov would prove to be a formidable adversary.

Barbatov began by asking Masterkov whether the reports he had authored and placed in the investigative file correctly represented his contact with Mr. Haynes.

Masterkov's answer was a simple "Yes, that is correct."

Barbatov then asked, "Did you follow all of the Constitutional and Criminal Procedure Code requirements in your dealing with Mr. Haynes?"

Again, Masterkov answered, "Yes, I did."

Barbatov then said, "And, finally, is your statement in your report dated 28 January 2006, and I quote, 'All the investigation in this case was done in accordance with constitutional and criminal code procedures,' intended to cover everything you did in that case?"

Again, Masterkov replied crisply, "Yes, that is the intent of the statement in the report."

"Your Honor, that completes my examination of Investigator Masterkov. You now have all the information you need. All of the correct procedures were followed. Investigator Masterkov, please return to your seat," Barbatov stated confidently.

Chávez interjected immediately. "Your Honor, I am sure Mr. Barbatov misspoke. I am sure he just overlooked my opportunity to question Investigator Masterkov."

"I doubt Mr. Barbatov overlooked anything, Mr. Chávez," Judge Vasilyuk retorted with a certain edginess to his voice.

"You have no such right, Mr. Chávez. It is completely up to me whether to allow any witness to testify in a proceeding, and completely up to me whether you get to ask any questions.

"Mr. Chávez, you have impressed me with your knowledge of the Russian Constitution and Russian procedures. However, our systems are not analogous, and you don't seem to understand that."

Chávez had to admit Vasilyuk was no fool. The rebuke had been delivered expertly. "Thank you, Your Honor. I seek only the rights my client is entitled to under Russian law. Article 123 of the Russian Constitution states that Russia shall use an adversarial system of justice, and parties to cases shall be equal before the court. An adversarial system of justice as defined anywhere in the world means that each side must have an equal opportunity to develop the facts of the case. To do so means that any witness should be subject to questioning by both sides."

Vasilyuk interjected again, "Don't lecture me, Mr. Chávez. You are a guest here. I intended to permit you to ask some questions of the investigator. You may do so now."

Chávez did not wait for more. "Investigator Masterkov, you could have had my client taken into custody in Seattle?"

Barbatov was on his feet instantly, shouting, "Objection, Your Honor. That's a leading question."

"I know it's a leading question, Your Honor. I am cross-examining the investigator," Chávez shot back, astonished by the objection. Katya had warned him about the problem; however, he just didn't think it was possible.

"Objection sustained," Vasilyuk said forcefully. "Again, Mr. Chávez, you appear not to understand. Our code does not permit leading questions. We seek the truth. Any question asked a witness at any stage of a proceeding must be open-ended, permitting a witness to fully explain. Your American trial techniques obscuring the truth through leading questions will not be permitted here. Please rephrase your question."

Chávez had read the article in the Criminal Procedure Code prohibiting leading questions, but that had to do with the interrogation of a suspect. Chávez could not understand how the Russian courts had determined that that rule also applied to court proceedings. He had to admit, however, it was their country, and he had to conform. Chávez rephrased the question. "Could you have had my client arrested by the FBI in Seattle?"

"No," Masterkov replied, "Russia has no extradition treaty with America."

For an instant, Chávez pondered the answer. Masterkov had given an accurate statement, but not a complete one. "Do Russian and American federal law enforcement personnel have a cooperation agreement?"

"Yes, that is correct."

"Through that agreement, could American law enforcement have questioned Mr. Haynes in connection with the investigation?"

"I don't know," Masterkov answered, "I have never asked anyone in the FBI to do that."

"At some point in your investigation, did you learn that Mr. Haynes had a return airline ticket?"

"Yes."

"How did you obtain that information?"

This time Masterkov paused, apparently waiting for Barbatov to object. When Barbatov remained silent, Masterkov turned and faced Judge Vasilyuk and asserted, "Your Honor, I decline to answer the question. As you know, our office has certain investigative methods that are confidential. This is one of those methods."

Before Chávez could frame a response Judge Vasilyuk ruled, "I agree. Mr. Chávez, that information is protected from disclosure. Please ask another question."

Chávez had to agree, and the answer was not important to the outcome of the hearing. Quickly he asked. "When did you learn that information?"

"A few days after Olga Sergova's murder."

"Was there time for you to have contacted the FBI and have them question Mr. Haynes in Seattle, Washington, before he returned to Sakhalin?"

"Yes, that could have been done, although as I said earlier, I have never contacted the American FBI. I doubt Mr. Haynes would have returned to Russia had he been contacted by the FBI in Seattle."

"Did you prefer to interrogate Mr. Haynes here in Russia, away from family, friends, or anyone that could be of immediate help?" Masterkov did not answer immediately, apparently waiting for Barbatov to object to the question. But no objection came from Barbatov's side of the room.

"Yes."

Chávez was surprised by Masterkov's answer. He was convinced Masterkov could have formulated a very credible response that did not agree with the inquiry. Perhaps Masterkov had his own agenda. "Thank you, Investigator. Let me turn to your actual contact with Mr. Haynes. Did you monitor Mr. Haynes' travel from Seattle to Sakhalin?"

"Yes."

"So you were aware that he had been traveling for more than thirty hours when he arrived in Sakhalin?"

"Yes."

Chávez found Masterkov's answers refreshingly candid. He was used to police witnesses in America. Though honest for the most part, they rarely agreed with the questions put to them by defense attorneys. Nearly always a police witness would attempt an innocent explanation for every contested matter even when it did not matter. It was obvious to Chávez that Masterkov was capable of such a response, but instead was responding directly to his questions. Masterkov's candid, direct responses were like many things in Russia, unexpected. "Does your report state when and what words you used to advise Mr. Haynes that he had the right to remain silent or the right to contact a lawyer?"

"No. However, I advised Mr. Haynes as follows: 'You are not required to answer. You have a right to the assistance of a lawyer.' I gave him that advice soon after I processed Mr. Haynes into the Detention Center."

Masterkov's answer demonstrated, despite his apparent candor, just how difficult it would be to control him. Just when Chávez thought Masterkov would give a simple yes or no answer, he had changed course. Nevertheless, Chávez had no choice but to press forward. "Did you advise Mr. Haynes of his rights under the Criminal Procedure Code?"

"Yes."

"Did that include the right to remain silent and the right to the assistance of counsel?"

"Yes."

"Did you advise him in Russian or English?"

"English."

"So, you speak English?"

"Yes."

"Tell us, in English, what words you used to advise Mr. Haynes."

"Mr. Haynes, silent you may remain, a right that you have, the lawyer right is also available to you." The translator then accurately restated Masterkov's English answer into Russian for Judge Vasilyuk and Barbatov. Although he would argue otherwise, Chávez thought that Masterkov's English was sufficient to convey the message and satisfy the Russian Constitution and the Criminal Procedure Code.

"Who else was in the room when you gave this advice to Mr. Haynes?"

"No one."

"Did you ever provide Mr. Haynes with an interpreter?"

"No."

"Was anyone else ever present in the room when you interrogated Mr. Haynes?"

"No one."

Chávez then changed course. "Are you familiar with the Vienna Convention?"

"No."

"The Russian Constitution provides that you must honor international human rights norms."

"Is that a question?"

"Yes, please answer it."

"Yes, the Russian Constitution says that."

"Do you agree that the Vienna Convention required you to inform Mr. Haynes that he had a right to talk to someone at the U.S. Consulate before you questioned him?"

"I don't know anything about the Vienna Convention."

"Objection!" Barbatov shouted about three questions late. "Your Honor, this kind of questioning of Investigator Masterkov has no place in a Russian courtroom. What Mr. Chávez seeks to prove by asking the investigator these questions escapes me."

"Your Honor, certainly Mr. Barbatov is aware that Russia is a signatory to the Vienna Convention, and the requirement in Article 36 that the authorities of the host nation—here that would be Russia—must inform a foreign national such as Mr. Haynes that he may speak to someone in his Consulate before being interrogated by the authorities of the host nation."

"I know of no such thing," Barbatov blurted out.

Apparently Judge Vasilyuk was not interested in hearing much more.

"Mr. Chávez, this is all very interesting, but for now, I don't think it is of much help to your client."

Chávez could tell it was time to move on, but he wanted to make one last point. He was now sure that he would not get Jonathan's alleged inculpatory statements excluded on these grounds. However, he wanted to rebut Vasilyuk's statements implying that he did not fully understand Russian law. "Your Honor, I understand. Let me just point out that Article 15(4) of the Russian Constitution requires that all Russian law conform to international human rights norms. The requirements of the Vienna Convention are some of those norms. The European Court of Human Rights and the International Justice Court have ruled that the rights under the Vienna Convention apply in a situation like this. I just want Your Honor to consider that fact as you determine whether to allow the jury to consider my client's alleged statements."

"Very well, I understand your point," Judge Vasilyuk replied.

Chávez had gone over the reports and the signed statement with Jonathan in great detail. Each time, Jonathan maintained that he really was not sure what he had signed. Jonathan had repeatedly told Chávez that, as the interrogation continued, he had become disoriented, perhaps more frightened than he had ever been in his life. Masterkov had continually told him things would be better for him if he signed the statement. It was now time to ask Masterkov about the actual statement.

"Investigator, you wrote this statement, not my client."

"Objection," Barbatov intoned.

Judge Vasilyuk leaned forward on the bench, "Mr. Chávez, please rephrase your question." Chávez made no argument in response. It was a leading question. The habit was hard to shake.

"Investigator, please tell us who wrote the words on this paper."

"I did."

Again, Chávez was impressed with Masterkov. He gave Chávez nothing but a small speck of the truth.

Chávez would have to work for everything. "Tell us how you came to write the statement."

"Mr. Haynes initially denied knowing Ms. Sergova. He did so numerous times. Then he admitted being with her on the night of December 20th. Eventually he admitted that he had gone to her apartment with her and had sexual intercourse with her. That is what I put down on the paper. I read to him what I had written, and he signed it."

Chávez listened intently to Masterkov's last narrative answer. Masterkov had just confirmed what Jonathan was trying to reconstruct from his disoriented state. He had not made the statement voluntarily. He had become so scared that he simply agreed to Masterkov's assertions. Masterkov's use of the Russian word for "admitted" was the key and gave Chávez a glimmer of hope for the trial.

"Please tell us what time it was when Mr. Haynes signed this statement," Chávez asked forcefully, his eyes locked on Masterkov.

Masterkov did not answer immediately. Chávez assumed he either was waiting for Barbatov to do something about the pending question or calculating his answer. No objection came from Barbatov's side of the table. "It was two a.m." Masterkov then replied directly.

Immediately Chávez asked, "And what time did his flight arrived in Sakhalin?"

Again, Masterkov hesitated slightly and then replied. "About eleven a.m."

"So it was more than twelve hours, and therefore you violated Article 46 of the Criminal Procedure Code requiring you to notify a relative of a suspect within twelve hours after a suspect is taken into custody."

Barbatov sprang to his feet. "Objection, he is asking leading questions again. He is spouting Russian law that he knows nothing about. He must be stopped."

Before Judge Vasilyuk could respond, Chávez answered. "I am sorry, Your Honor, I got a bit carried away. I will rephrase. Investigator Masterkov, did you contact a lawyer for Mr. Haynes within twelve hours of taking him into custody?"

Masterkov's face gave no hint of concern despite what Chávez thought would prove to be a violation of the Criminal Procedure Code. "No, Mr. Haynes could only provide me with a phone number for his boss at Exxon. I tried the cell number but only got a voice mail. Mr. Haynes did not ask for a lawyer, and it was a Saturday night. There were no lawyers available."

"So my client had been up for forty hours, had not talked to anyone at the U.S. Consulate, and had no opportunity to speak to a lawyer when you shoved the paper in front of him."

"Objection," Barbatov intoned.

Again Chávez apologized. "Sorry, Your Honor, let me try again. Investigator Masterkov, do you know what time Mr. Haynes' plane left Seattle, Washington, then Seoul, Korea?"

Masterkov simply said, "Yes, I do."

Inwardly Chávez respected the simple answer that really was the correct answer. "Could you please give us those times?"

"Yes. Mr. Haynes' KAL flight left Seattle at nine p.m. Western Pacific time, arrived in Seoul at five-thirty a.m., and the flight from Seoul left at eight-thirty a.m. in our time zone."

"Please tell us Mr. Haynes' emotional state at two a.m. when you put the piece of paper in front of him."

Again, in a clear voice, Masterkov replied, "He was emotionally upset by his circumstances, as all criminals are when they are caught. It is quite common really."

A skillful answer, Chávez thought. Now it seemed the police were the same in every courtroom in the world. It was as if Masterkov was playing a game. If you ask a question that can be answered precisely, you will get a precise answer. However, if a question is imprecise the answers will be shaped in a way that hurts the questioner. Nevertheless, Chávez needed to ask one more question. "Investigator Masterkov, at what time in this over-twelve-hour interrogation did my client urinate on himself?"

Barbatov sprang from his chair. "He's leading again."

Masterkov ignored Barbatov. "Mr. Chávez, at about one a.m. I noticed that your client had urinated on himself. There was a puddle on the floor. I don't know when he actually did it."

It was time to stop. Chávez knew he was not going to get the statement excluded. There was no reason to reveal anything more to Barbatov. He would save the other crucial facts about Masterkov's interrogation techniques for the jury. "Thank you, Investigator. I have no more questions."

As Masterkov began to leave the witness podium, Chávez turned back toward him. "Excuse me, Your Honor. I do have one more question for Investigator Masterkov."

Barbatov jumped up screaming, "It's over, what's he doing?"

As Barbatov screamed, Chávez asked his last question loudly, "Investigator, did you take possession of my client's cell phone as soon as you arrested him?"

Masterkov did not answer the question. Instead he waited as Judge Vasilyuk ruled the question out of order. Although Masterkov did not answer the question, Chávez was sure Masterkov understood the implication of the question.

That skirmish over, Judge Vasilyuk permitted the lawyers to make brief legal arguments.

Judge Vasilyuk did not hesitate. As soon as Chávez completed his argument, Vasilyuk ruled. "I am not sure that the Constitution applies to someone who is not a Russian citizen. In any event, no rights under the Russian Constitution or the Russian Criminal Procedure Code were violated. That includes the Vienna Convention issue. The signature on the statement was the defendant's, and the statement was given voluntarily. The statement will remain in the investigative file. The jury will be permitted to consider the statement."

Chávez had not really expected to get the statement excluded. He had, however, accomplished one of his goals—to get Masterkov on the stand and test him. As he walked from the courtroom Chávez was sure of one thing: Masterkov would play a big role in determining whether Jonathan Haynes went home or died in a Russian prison.

CHAPTER

18

Masterkov felt a sense of relief the moment that Chávez finished questioning him. Although he had not been concerned that Judge Vasilyuk would invalidate Haynes' statement, the experience in court with Chávez was nevertheless punishing. He would have to work hard to stay ahead of Chávez. It was obvious that Chávez was skilled and becoming comfortable in a Russian courtroom.

More disturbing, however, was the thought that Chávez was inspiring the local defense bar through his use of the adversarial reforms that were now part of the Constitution and the Criminal Procedure Code. The courtroom had been packed with Sakhalin defense lawyers. Before long all the defense lawyers on Sakhalin would be filing such motions.

Then there was the question regarding Haynes' cell phone. Masterkov would need to inform Karpov and Barbatov that Haynes' cell phone was missing. Masterkov put that thought behind him as he entered his apartment. Inside, he poured himself a glass of Georgian wine and turned his attention to Ivan Dudinov.

Masterkov had been interested in Dudinov's various entrepreneurial activities for a couple of years. Dudinov imported used cars from Japan, had an interest in Yuzhno's largest taxi company, and owned the Grey Kat bar. Dudinov's car business brought him to Masterkov's attention. It was Olga Sergova who had first told him that Dudinov had close ties to certain customs officials who often failed to record and charge the proper import duty and other fees on all of Dudinov's cars.

Although that investigation went nowhere, Masterkov had learned some interesting facts about Dudinov in the process. As with many things Russian, Dudinov's past revealed a complex image. Dudinov had spent nearly twenty-five years in the Russian Army. He had survived the Russian debacle in Afghanistan as a highly-decorated infantry commander. After Afghanistan, he moved to more clandestine work with a Russian special forces unit. It was in Chechnya, however, where Dudinov's army career had ended. Although the information was incomplete, Masterkov had concluded that Dudinov had been in command of the unit allegedly responsible for the slaughter of an entire Chechnyan village. Three years after that incident Dudinov had arrived on Sakhalin, a civilian. Based on Dudinov's past and his activities on Sakhalin, Masterkov had decided he was worth keeping an eye on. One of Masterkov's informants had witnessed the meeting between Chávez and Dudinov in the Grey Kat.

Masterkov closed his eyes and considered the problems that Dudinov brought to the case. First, Masterkov doubted that Chávez understood the complexity of Russian life and what Chávez would likely encounter by associating himself with a man like Dudinov who operated in and out of the island's criminal milieu.

Second, Dudinov could just pocket Chávez's money and eventually report to Chávez that there was nothing he could find that would be helpful to Jonathan Haynes. As unfair as it seemed, that was the outcome Masterkov preferred—the outcome that was likely the safest for everyone in the case.

Third, it was possible that Dudinov had connections and influence that might turn up people or things inconsistent with what appeared on the surface to be an ironclad case against Haynes. Having just experienced Chávez in court, Masterkov was sure that Chávez was capable of exploiting even the tiniest fact that was inconsistent with the case against Jonathan Haynes.

Immediately after being informed that Chávez had met Dudinov at the Grey Kat, Masterkov had one of his operatives install a tiny directional tracking device, operating the latest GPS technology, underneath Dudinov's expensive Lexus SUV.

Although the evidence of Haynes' guilt was intact so far, Masterkov had to protect himself from the unforeseen. Although Chávez was handicapped in many ways—some ways Chávez was conscious of, some he had no inkling of—their most recent encounter demonstrated that, in a courtroom, Chávez was a dangerous adversary. In combination, Chávez and Dudinov had the means to cause trouble. There was no doubt in Masterkov's mind that if anything went wrong in the case, Karpov would see that Masterkov was the sacrificial lamb.

Masterkov now watched in fascination as three days' worth of information from the tracking device appeared on his home computer screen. As he had expected, Dudinov spent a good deal of time in his car, moving about the city between his upscale apartment and his three businesses.

The computer mapping information revealed an unremarkable routine for the first thirty-six hours after the device had been installed. Nothing out of the ordinary—then things changed. On the evening of the second day, the tracking device revealed that Dudinov had traveled to three different sectors of the city. In each sector his car had stopped near a bar. Each bar was already on Masterkov's watch list as a haven of criminal activity mostly associated with disaffected war veterans, all of them either alcoholics or drug abusers.

Then, on the evening of the third day, Dudinov had left the city driving north about thirty miles toward a small village. Dudinov had stayed in the village for nearly three hours. Masterkov sensed there was something important there, and he needed to know about it as soon as possible.

CHAPTER

19

A bitter-cold wind penetrated Chávez's heavy wool jacket and corduroy pants as he stood in front of the Sapporo waiting in the fading afternoon light for Dudinov to pick him up. Everything was gray: the tired old buildings visible in each direction, the piles of dirty snow that lined the streets, all of it was gray. And that included most of the people that he saw bundled up moving along the street. Yuzhno, despite being surrounded by physical beauty in all directions, seemed clinically depressed. Were it not for Katya, a similar gray mood would have completely consumed him. All that Dudinov said in the brief phone conversation was that he had found a possible witness in a village to the north.

Within minutes Dudinov emerged from the afternoon traffic and Chávez jumped in the left front passenger door. His eyes immediately focused on the nine-milimeter Makarov visible inside Dudinov's fleeced-lined leather jacket.

Two thoughts quickly passed through Chávez's head. No one in the world knew that Chávez was heading into the Russian hinterland with Dudinov, a man he hardly knew or had any reason to trust. Katya was in Vladivostok on another case. Chávez wondered if the Makarov was to protect Dudinov and himself, or was it for something else? Within minutes, Dudinov's Lexus was already near the northern reaches of the city. To Chávez it felt like a point of no return.

Dudinov drove fast for the road conditions, weaving past the more obvious potholes and other indentations visible in the snow-covered road. Frequently, Dudinov looked in the rearview mirror. Chávez looked in the side mirror at a black SUV that seemed to be taking the same route out of the city.

Near the outskirts of the city, Chávez began to see ramshackle wooden dwellings that appeared barely erect. There was smoke coming from the chimneys of most of the houses. Seeking to break the silence, Chávez asked in Russian, "Are these small houses dachas?"

"No," Dudinov replied abruptly, not taking his eyes from the road.

"Oh, then do these people travel into the city to work?" Chávez asked.

"No, most of them do not work in the city. These people do not have jobs as you Americans think of a job. They simply exist," Dudinov replied. This time, however, he glanced sideways as he answered Chávez's question.

They had cleared the outskirts of the city and sped along in silence as Chávez took in the snowy countryside and speculated whether the poor souls living in the country had enough heat or running water. After another five minutes of silence, with the black SUV still visible in the fading light some distance behind them, Chávez asked, "Ivan, where are we heading exactly?"

"We are going to a village about thirty minutes north of the city," Dudinov answered, his eyes repeatedly checking the rearview mirror. "There's a guy I want you to talk to. I found him last night. I am in contact with some Chechnya veterans scattered around the island. Some are getting along better than others. Afghanistan and Chechnya were rough, especially for the young guys who served in Chechnya. I found this guy last night. He told me that he was approached by a man—he thinks it was in November last year. The man said he was interested in having him do a job. The offer was $10,000 U.S. The job involved a woman on Sakhalin. He thinks the man said she was a television reporter or a newspaper reporter."

Chávez's heart started to beat rapidly. "Could he have murdered Sergova?" Chávez asked too quickly.

Dudinov did not answer. Instead, he abruptly turned off the main road toward a small village. The road was more narrow but passable. To Chávez's relief the car that had been behind them since they left the city did not turn at the village sign.

Chávez was surprised to see an apartment building in the village. Dudinov, instead of answering the pending question, explained that many apartments were built in the villages during Soviet times. The Chechnya veteran lived in one.

The veteran's building was in even greater disrepair than the ones Chávez had observed in the city. As they got closer to the building Chávez realized that the apartment's foundation had settled at one end and that the five story structure was noticeably askew. They entered through a large outer metal door. The hallway was pitch black. Dudinov pulled out a small flashlight, turned it on, and guided Chávez to a main hallway. Dudinov stopped at the fifth door on the right and banged loudly with his left foot. Dudinov's right hand was near the Makarov. There was no response.

He called out, "Sergei, it's Dudinov, open the door."

Chávez heard some movement, and the door opened slightly, then all the way.

Sergei Egorov had a bandana on his head, covering most of his sandy colored hair. He had on a wrinkled shirt and older military-style camouflage pants. Chávez estimated his height at about six feet. Sergei had a reddish birthmark that ran down a portion of the left side of his forehead and a thin pointed face. His nose was large and shaped like an Indian arrowhead.

To Chávez's surprise, Sergei greeted Dudinov in a friendly manner. Chávez resisted the urge to look around the room. Instead, he tried to move his eyes imperceptibly. There was a cot to one side with a blanket, but no other visible bedding. A small sink was located in one corner and a hot plate was on a grimy table near the sink. On the table were small boxes of food items, such as crackers and smoked fish. A portable heater was operating in another corner of the room. An open bottle of vodka was visible on another table.

Dudinov got right to business, introducing Chávez and recounting the events that had brought the three of them together. Sergei's replies to Dudinov's questions revealed that Sergei was sober. He denied killing Sergova.

Dudinov then turned to Chávez indicating it was his turn to speak.

Chávez looked directly at Sergei. "Thanks for talking to me."

Sergei did not reply; instead he poured vodka into three small tin cups and motioned for Chávez and Dudinov to pull chairs to the small table.

Once they were seated, Sergei offered the cup to Chávez, exclaiming, "*Choot, Choot.*" Chávez understood the Russian connotation, "Let's have a small drink."

Chávez looked at the tin cup brimming with vodka. He knew that Sergei would watch how quickly he drank the vodka. Chávez had no fear of downing the vodka. Instead, he feared the cup, wondering when it had last been washed. Hoping the alcohol would kill the worst of the germs, he picked up the cup and drained it completely. A slight smile crossed Sergei's thin lips. Chávez knew that he had passed an initial test.

Chávez decided to start with questions that any prosecutor was likely to ask, should Sergei ever be a witness. "I think that the first thing I need to know is why you were contacted about a contract murder."

Sergei smiled slightly and glanced at Dudinov. "I have no idea. About a year ago a couple of guys from my unit in Chechnya were asked to do a job like that. Maybe my name came up."

Chávez had no way of assessing the accuracy of Sergei's response. However, the benign nature of the answer revealed that Sergei had some brain cells left and might make a decent witness, if things ever got that far. "Did they do the job?"

Sergei shrugged, "They left the island soon after that."

"Tell me what you remember about the contact."

Sergei again looked at Dudinov. Dudinov said nothing, and no sign appeared on Dudinov's face.

"OK, ah, I was sitting at the bar by myself, and this guy sat down next to me. He asked if I was looking to score a lot of money. I said that depends. He showed me a photo of a woman and said that she needed to disappear."

A photo. Chávez's heart again started to race. It was consistent with what the madam at the Eurasia had told Dudinov. The Georgian had a photo. Chávez was sure, however, that Sergei was not Georgian.

"Do you remember the woman in the picture?"

Sergei paused and looked around the room. "Yes, I am positive it was the Sergova woman. But, like I said, I was fucked up."

"Did he give you the photo?"

Again Sergei paused. Chávez could tell that Sergei was smart enough to understand the significance of his next answer. Eventually, Sergei responded, "Yeah, he gave it to me."

"So you agreed to do it?"

"Well, sort of. He said he would get back in touch with me, and give me half of the money, $5,000 U.S. dollars. The remainder would be paid after I did the job."

"Did he say why he wanted the woman in the photo to disappear?"

"Not really, but I got the feeling she was some kind of television reporter or something like that. And that she was causing some trouble."

"Do you still have the photo?"

"No, Ivan asked me for it also. I lost it somewhere, I guess."

Chávez tried not to show his disappointment. "Were you ever contacted by this man again?"

"I gave the guy my cell phone number, but he never called."

"Were you going to murder Sergova?"

Sergei looked over at Dudinov, who nodded perceptibly. With a slight smile Sergei answered. "No. I was going to get the first half of the money and take off."

"Can you describe the man who contacted you?"

"Not really. You know, it was dark. He had a beard, dark hair, fat."

"Had you ever seen him before?"

"Not that I can think of. You know, people come and go in those bars in Yuzhno."

Still thinking that, if everything failed, he might be able to argue to the jury that Sergei Egorov could have been the murderer and that that possibility alone was enough to create reasonable doubt. However, in order to make that a plausible claim Chávez had to ask another very direct question. "Sergei, do you have some sort of alibi in the case the Prokuror becomes interested in you?"

Again Sergei glanced at Dudinov, and smiled as he answered. "Ah, yes, ah I was in the Detention Center the last two weeks of December and the first week of January." This time it was Chávez's turn to smile. He had to admit that was about as good an alibi as you get, assuming it was the truth.

Chávez had asked enough questions. Sergei's answers were detailed enough to be meaningful in court. And there was Egorov's claim that he had been given a photo of Sergova, matching the claim by the mythical Tatiana that her customer also had a photo of Sergova. As Chávez and Dudinov drove back to Yuzhno, Dudinov explained that he understood from news reports about other contract murders that there were often multiple solicitations preceding the actual murder. In Dudinov's opinion the Sergova murder might fit that pattern. Chávez was silent a good deal of the way back to Yuzhno pondering whether Sergei's answers were actually Sergei's, or whether Dudinov had orchestrated the whole thing.

CHAPTER

20

Masterkov walked briskly down the corridor toward Karpov's office. He cautioned himself as he did before each meeting with Karpov; listen to the questions and assume Karpov knows the answer to each question he is asking.

This time Karpov was already at his desk, sipping tea and looking down at some papers, when his secretary announced Masterkov's entry.

"Good morning, Alexander Sergeevich," Karpov said, glancing up from his papers.

"Good morning, sir," Masterkov replied as the secretary placed a steaming cup of tea in front of him.

"Alexander Sergeevich, I assume that you are aware that Ivan Dudinov, an ex-special forces officer, is somehow involved in the Haynes case?"

That abrupt assertion told Masterkov that Karpov was armed with information and meant business this morning. "Yes, I know Dudinov is involved." Masterkov replied. He did not intend to volunteer anything.

"I assume you are watching him."

"Yes, General. I have informants in the city who are keeping track of him."

"I see," Karpov said slowly.

"So, what is he doing?" Karpov continued almost matter of factly.

"Not so much. He has moved about the city, mostly talking to criminals in bars. Nothing specific," Masterkov replied, realizing he may have answered too quickly.

Karpov pounced. "You did not know he had been out of the city?"

Masterkov knew he had miscalculated. With Karpov, even the most innocuous question had a purpose. Karpov was watching Dudinov. But why? He did not have time to figure it out. He needed to respond immediately. "I am sorry, General. I should have explained more thoroughly. Yes, Dudinov has been to that small village north of the city. He has been there twice. The second time he brought Chávez. He met with a Chechnyan veteran who lives there. The man's name is Sergei Egorov. He's a drunk and a junky. I have searched his apartment. I found nothing having anything to do with the Haynes case."

"Have you talked to the man?" Karpov interrupted.

"No, General, as I was about to say, I don't want Dudinov to know we are watching him," Masterkov replied.

"Of course," Karpov shot back.

"Do you know why Dudinov and Chávez are talking to this man?"

"No," Masterkov replied, not completely truthfully. He suspected he knew why Dudinov was talking to veterans of Chechnya, and he suspected that Karpov thought the same thing. However, to Masterkov's surprise, Karpov did not press him for any further details regarding Dudinov.

"Alexander, keep me informed of Dudinov's movements. As I have told you repeatedly, we can't have any surprises," Karpov concluded, moving on to a new topic. "Alexander, here is a list of the people who have returned juror summons. Let's find out about them."

Karpov had obviously breached any security the court was supposed to exercise regarding the list of potential jurors. Why should Masterkov be surprised? "Yes, of course," Masterkov stated.

Karpov picked up the cell phone on his desk signaling that the meeting was over.

Masterkov did not return to his own office; instead, he left the building. He had to get away from Karpov's presence. Now Karpov wanted him to check the backgrounds of all the potential jurors. He had to think. Karpov obviously had his own operatives devoted to the case, including surveilling Dudinov. Was Karpov just concerned about winning the case, or was his personal involvement motivated by something different? Whatever was the truth, Masterkov had to conclude that Karpov likely had agents also watching him.

CHAPTER
21

Chávez was alone in every way possible. Dudinov had reported that he had not located or obtained any further information he could trust on the the hooker Tatiana, assuming that she even existed. Dudinov also had reported that the Kurilova woman no longer lived in her apartment and that he was working hard to find her. The day before Masterkov had filed a new report for the investigative file stating that Jonathan's cell phone could not be located in the evidence locker. Not even a sliver of evidence remained corroborating Jonathan's claim that he and Sergova had been dating for months before her murder. And there was little likelihood that Judge Vasilyuk would do anything about it. The kinds of procedural remedies for lost evidence that were commonplace in American criminal procedure—dismissal of the charge or requiring the prosecution to stipulate to the favorable evidence—simply did not exist in the newly developed Russian law on criminal procedure. Sergei Egorov represented the only glimmer of hope—a screwed-up war veteran who claimed that someone he could describe only as a dark-haired fat guy with a beard, had offered him

$10,000 to murder Sergova. It would take more than a miracle for Judge Vasilyuk to permit Egorov to testify.

Chávez's judgeship was clearly at risk. Articles had appeared in *The Oregonian*, *The New York Times*, and *The Washington Post* describing Chávez's involvement in a Russian murder case. Senator Garlock had made it very clear in a strained conversation the evening before that there could be no postponements of the Senate Judiciary Committee hearing. Garlock emphasized that Chávez was one of the few nominees for the federal bench that the Democrats would allow to have a hearing—Chávez could not risk a postponement. The hearing was scheduled for March 20. He had to be in Washington, D.C. a week before the hearing to meet with each of the senators on the Senate Judiciary Committee and to prepare for the hearing. Everything in Russia had to be resolved in two weeks.

Chávez's mind raced from the evening telephone call back to the present. He was in a Russian courtroom about to begin selecting a jury. Familiar feelings of regret, feelings that he had not done enough, that he had not been smart enough, overtook him. These feelings threatened him before every major trial. Usually, he could repress them by methodically concentrating on the trial tasks immediately in front of him. This time, however, it was different. As much as he tried, he could not focus. He could have avoided all of it—he could have stayed home.

Like a slide show running too fast, his mind flipped through events that had led him to this unfamiliar courtroom on the other side of the world, involved in a case that he was sure he did not yet truly understand and for which he had no real defense.

Three slides ran together; suddenly he saw the powerful black arms that had lifted him to safety in Vietnam, then he saw Michael Haynes wearing the oxygen pack, and then he saw an image of Jonathan Haynes dead in a frozen Russian prison.

Two more slides shot through his brain. He and Claire together at home, secure in their nearly three-decade-long embrace. However, in an instant his mental image of Claire transformed to Katya.

Barbatov's clamorous entry into the courtroom jolted Chávez out of the slide show. Katya entered behind Barbatov. In the next instant the door to Judge Vasilyuk's chambers opened. As soon as he took the bench, Vasilyuk motioned to one of the bailiffs who opened a door on the other side of the courtroom. Through that door stepped thirty Yuzhno residents. As each potential juror came through the door they looked in one direction. Not toward the judge or the lawyers. Instead, each potential juror stared directly at the tall, very skinny young black man standing in the cage across from them.

Chávez was not surprised—a black man caged in a Russian courtroom would certainly provoke powerful emotions in the xenophobic Russians. For two evenings he and Katya had tested the case on eight carefully-selected Yuzhno residents—a technique Chávez always used in big cases in the U.S. His fears about his client's race had been confirmed. However, not all the news was bad.

Interviews and discussions those two evenings revealed that Yuzhno residents were, like most former Soviet citizens, generally distrustful of government at all levels. They were unfamiliar with courts. During Soviet times, only bad things happened to people in a court-room. No Soviet citizen would have turned to a court to solve a legal dispute. They understood the idea of false confessions. That general distrust of the government was the good news. However, if not overtly hostile to black-skinned foreigners, Yuzhno residents were, at a mini-mum, uncomfortable with them in their midst. Katya's law firm had provided a number of news articles about racially-motivated assaults in Yuzhno during the last five years. That was the bad news.

For an instant Chávez reflected on Katya's admonition that jury service in Russia was considered a privilege and not an obligation as it was in the United States. Still, Chávez found it disturbing that of the one hundred jury summons that had been sent out, only thirty had been returned. That was only ten more than the minimum required to com-mence a trial under the Russian Criminal Procedure Code. It had been more than ten years since the jury trial had been reintroduced in Russia. Chávez would need to find out why these thirty people were willing to spend time away from their jobs when seventy others apparently were not. Each side would have several peremptory challenges, or as the Russians called them, "unmotivated," challenges, that could be exercised to remove undesirable jurors. The unmotivated challenges were exercised in writing, and therefore the remaining jurors could only speculate about which side had exercised the challenge.

Ultimately, fourteen jurors would be seated—twelve plus two alternates. Not that different from the American system. At the end of the trial, the jury would be asked to answer three questions "yes" or "no": Whether the act that was the subject of the charge occurred, whether that act was committed by the defendant, and whether the defendant was guilty of committing the offense. Chávez did not see the need for the third question. How could a jury answer "yes" to the first two questions, but "no" to the third question? Katya had explained that the third question was part of the original jury trial system that had existed in Russia from 1864 until the revolution. It was the third question that permitted jury nullification—the ability of a jury to tell the government that, although the defendant may have broken the law, the law should not be enforced against that defendant.

Unlike the American system that had no time limit, a Russian jury would first be given three hours to reach a unanimous decision. However, if unanimity could not be achieved in that time, then a simple majority would be sufficient to convict, or a not-guilty verdict would result when at least six jurors answered "no" to one of the questions. Chávez remained unsure whether the Russian method favored the prosecutor or the defense.

Judge Vasilyuk spent about an hour with his preliminary questions to the jury panel. To Chávez, however, it seemed that in an instant Vasilyuk turned to him and directed him to begin questioning the first juror.

Juror number one, Mr. Panokov, was short with a slightly oval face and a full head of prematurely white hair. The gap between Mr. Panokov's front teeth seemed to dominate his appearance due to the wide smile that was a permanent part of Mr. Panokov's countenance.

Chávez began, "Good morning, Mr. Panokov. How are you this morning?

CHAPTER

22

Masterkov had arrived early and seated himself in a corner of the courtroom. From that vantage point he could hear each of Chávez's questions, the jurors' answers, and also observe the jurors' facial reactions and body language as they answered Chávez. Masterkov glanced at his watch, surprised that it was nearly four o'clock. He had lost track of time in the morning and now again in the afternoon. Despite his efforts to the contrary, Masterkov had become transfixed by the competence, the charm, and the air of confidence that Chávez exuded as he questioned each juror. Chávez's Russian now seemed impeccable. Barbatov, however, armed with the secret investigation of the potential jurors that Masterkov had supervised, asked few questions. That was probably the best decision Barbatov had made in the courtroom in some time—what questions he did ask were generally meaningless.

As with many American legal topics and procedures, the Internet had provided Masterkov with valuable insights into the jury selection process that American lawyers described in French as *voir dire*. Particularly valuable, however, was the transcript of a model *voir dire* examination that Masterkov had found on the Oregon District Attorneys Association website. Apparently, Oregon prosecutors considered the defense lawyer's questioning technique in that case so good that it was likely other defense lawyers would adopt the same style and technique. The prosecutors had to be ready. Masterkov could not help but chuckle when he discovered halfway down the first transcript page that the defense lawyer was Peter Chávez.

Masterkov provided the model *voir dire* to Barbatov who demonstrated not the slightest interest in it. After all, the jury selection would not be fair; Barbatov was armed with Masterkov's secret investigation.

Chávez's technique, adapted to the eccentricities of Russian criminal procedure, appeared to Masterkov every bit as effective as the examinations featured in the transcript on the Internet. Chávez's tone with each juror was conversational. His sentences, constructed in perfect Russian, were short, but pointed. The questions were open-ended—a juror could not determine a right, wrong, or expected answer. Through a variety of seemingly unrelated topics, jurors revealed their views about the government and the police, the unsolved murders of fourteen other Russian journalists, race relations in Russia, attitudes toward Americans, attitudes and connections to the large oil and gas ventures on Sakhalin, and a variety of other queries, all apparently designed to reveal perceptions and thoughts that Masterkov simply could not always follow.

What impressed Masterkov even more was that Chávez had done it so quickly. The final juror would be selected by the end of the day.

Masterkov again reviewed the list of potential jurors and the information that had been compiled on each of them. Chávez had discovered and removed from the first twelve that had been seated two of the three jurors that Masterkov knew the prosecution could count on to vote guilty regardless of the evidence.

Chávez was not perfect, however. He had allowed juror number ten, the woman law professor and former prosecutor, to remain on the jury. Although her answers appeared careful and thoughtful, Chávez managed to get her to reveal her bias against the legal-democratic reforms that were now a part of Russian law. Yet Chávez had left her on the jury. In Masterkov's view the woman was by far the strongest personality on the jury, would be the foreperson, and would undoubtedly deliver the necessary guilty verdict. Still, Chávez's decision to leave her on the jury was perplexing. Was it possible there was something about the professor helpful to the defense that only Chávez understood?

CHAPTER

23

Chávez arrived at the hotel dining room at six a.m., just as it opened. He had spent the first part of the previous evening with Katya reviewing the jury selection. Katya's only disagreement was with his decision to leave the woman law professor on the jury. Chávez tried to respond confidently to Katya, but inside he knew it was a risky choice. He believed that the law professor was the subject of an anonymous hotel room voicemail indicating that, despite what might be said during jury selection, there was a woman among the group of potential jurors who would be a good juror for the defense. The professor's answers created the impression that she was not a big fan of the jury reforms. Chávez concluded, however, that her eyes, which focused directly on Chávez's eyes as she answered the questions, signaled otherwise. He had decided not to tell Katya about the voicemail. Time would tell. He had spent the remainder of the evening in his hotel room preparing his opening statement.

Over breakfast he put the finishing touches on his opening statement; then he walked to the courthouse in a light snow that had been falling since midnight.

Dudinov had left a cell phone message stating that Jonathan's apartment in Nogliki had been stripped clean. Nothing remained in the apartment, not even Jonathan's clothes. No one seemed to know anything about Jonathan's possessions. Despite Dudinov's repeated assurances, Chávez remained skeptical whether Dudinov could produce the veteran Sergei Egorov for trial and doubtful that Judge Vasilyuk would let him put Egorov on the stand in front of the jury. Egorov's alibi had been confirmed by the detention center; he was not the contract killer. Chávez had wanted to talk to Sergova's friend and co-employee, Natalia Kurilova, before the trial began to discuss Sergova's investigation. Hopefully, Dudinov was close to finding Kurilova. For the first time in his life as a trial lawyer, Chávez had no real evidence to present. He suspected that this was what the defense encountered every day in the old Soviet system.

As Chávez entered the courtroom he observed that it was nearly full. Most of the spectators were foreign press and Sakhalin defense lawyers. Katya, already seated, looked up from her trial book and smiled but said nothing. Chávez and Katya had not touched since they had danced at the restaurant, after Judge Vasilyuk's ruling had seemingly condemned him to Sakhalin Island like one of the prisoners in Chekhov's book. Chávez picked up a chair and moved it from the counsel table to a place next to the cage holding Jonathan. The guard at the cage said nothing. He would have to place his yellow tablet on his knees to take notes. That seemed to be the only way to converse with Jonathan about events during the trial.

And it was one way to demonstrate for the jurors that Chávez cared about his client.

Within minutes, Judge Vasilyuk took the bench and called for the jurors. As soon as the jurors were in place Judge Vasilyuk signaled to Barbatov. Feeling as if he were somehow watching from afar, Chávez focused on Barbatov as he rose from his seat at counsel table and walked to the small podium facing the jury.

In accordance with Russian procedure Barbatov began by reading the voluminous accusatory instrument to the jury. In America the accusatory instrument, usually an indictment, would simply list the crime or crimes allegedly committed and a brief couple of sentences describing factually how the crimes were committed. Reading the indictment would generally take no more than a couple of minutes. However, under Russian procedure the accusatory instrument was generally a very lengthy document describing the charged crimes and setting out in detail what important witnesses said during the preliminary investigation that established the defendant's guilt. As Chávez listened to Barbatov read verbatim from the accusatory instrument Chávez began to realize for the first time how truly different were the American and Russian systems. In America pretrial investigation had little formality to it; much evidence, even some very relevant evidence, would never be heard by a jury. An American trial was all about formality intended to guarantee that a jury heard only evidence considered reliable under rules that had been hundreds of years in the making. However, in Russia the preliminary investigation was conducted under very formal rules, and therefore every aspect of the preliminary investigation was documented in excruciating detail, and it was the prosecutor's job to relate all of the information that was part of the preliminary investigation and the drafting of the accusatory instrument to the jury. It took Barbatov hours to do so. In reality a Russian criminal trial was simply another phase of the criminal investigation.

Although Barbatov droned on for hours, Chávez thought the jury would likely remember a few key points from Barbatov's opening statement beginning with, "Citizens of the jury, the defendant is an American oil worker. He is charged with the brutal rape and murder of Yuzhno resident Olga Sergova." Barbatov had then turned and glared at the cage. Jonathan looked away. Before Chávez could make eye contact with Barbatov, he had returned to his argument.

"Dr. Victor Mitrokhin performed an autopsy of Sergova's body. Dr. Mitrokhin found the defendant's semen in Sergova's vagina. That has been confirmed by DNA testing. Dr. Mitrokhin determined that Sergova's death was caused by manual strangulation, by a person whose hands were large and very powerful. The defendant is six-feet-four inches tall. He played basketball at an American university, and, as you will see, he has large hands. Dr. Mitrokhin determined that Olga Sergova was murdered sometime on the night of December 20th or the early morning hours of December 21st.

"Ms. Sergova's apartment was immediately examined for fingerprints. Boris Popov, one of our country's leading fingerprint experts, has positively identified a fingerprint found on a wine glass in Sergova's apartment as a print of the defendant's right index finger. The defendant was observed at the 777 Restaurant with Sergova on the night she was murdered."

Again Barbatov stopped and looked over to the cage. This time Chávez was ready. He stared directly at Barbatov. Their eyes locked on one another. Barbatov looked away and continued. "Citizens of the jury, the evidence that I have described so far is, by itself, enough to demonstrate positively and beyond a doubt that the defendant raped and murdered Ms. Sergova. There is more, however. After being taken into custody by Senior Investigator Alexander Sergeevich Masterkov, the defendant repeatedly lied to Investigator Masterkov, first claiming that he had never met Ms. Sergova. However, the defendant eventually admitted that he had been with her that evening, had gone to her apartment, and that he had sexual intercourse with her. In other words the defendant admitted to everything except putting his hands around her neck. If that were true the defendant had no reason to lie to Investigator Masterkov. Of course he lied because he knew he had strangled Ms. Sergova. At the end of the case, I will ask for your guilty verdict."

Despite its length Chávez considered Barbatov's opening statement a powerful one. Barbatov had clearly described the evidence establishing Jonathan's guilt. Although Barbatov was an experienced prosecutor; he was not, however, an experienced jury lawyer. As a holdover from the Soviet system, he was used to winning every case against weak opposition. An American prosecutor would never ignore any facts or circumstances that might support the defense. Instead, an

American prosecutor would rush to disclose those facts but then explain why they were unimportant or would be countered by other evidence. Barbatov never mentioned Jonathan's now-missing cell phone. A source inside the prosecutor's office had informed Katya that Masterkov was irate, had torn the evidence room apart, and was threatening an investigation over the missing cell phone.

Because lawyers in America have the power of subpoena, Chávez was used to knowing before trial which witnesses and physical evidence he could subpoena to court on a defendant's behalf. That kind of certainty and transparency simply was not present in the Russian criminal justice system. In Russia he could not anticipate how the evidence would unfold during the trial.

Chávez was uncertain which witnesses—if any—Judge Vasilyuk would permit him to question in front of the jury, or the latitude Vasilyuk would permit in the questioning of those witnesses. He had no idea whether Kurilova had anything to offer that might help the defense or whether he would have any opportunity to question her in court, assuming Dudinov could eventually locate her. As a result, Chávez had to use his opening statement to convey to the jury that Jonathan's guilt was far from certain, but it had to be done without much specificity.

First, however, Jonathan would address the jury. Unlike in America, where generally only the defendant's lawyer gives an opening statement, in Russia the defendant and his or her lawyer may both make an opening statement. Chávez and Jonathan had gone over Jonathan's prepared remarks numerous times during the last few days before the trial. They had decided on a short, concise approach. Jonathan would introduce himself, talk about his background, and then vehemently deny his guilt. Nevertheless, Chávez knew that Jonathan remained extremely apprehensive.

Chávez stood and informed Judge Vasilyuk and the jury that Jonathan would exercise his right to address the jury. Vasilyuk motioned to the guard, and the cage door opened. As Jonathan emerged from the cage, Chávez saw for just an instant, the image of Michael Haynes.

Jonathan, like his father, was not brown—he was black. He stood up straight, revealing as he walked to the podium his full six-foot-four-inch, but now very thin, frame. Although Jonathan's face exuded calm, Chávez saw the slight tremor in Jonathan's legs as he stood at the podium.

Jonathan started to speak; however, his voice was drowned out immediately by Judge Vasilyuk. Vasilyuk shouted at Jonathan and the interpreter to stop speaking. Vasilyuk had forgotten to advise Jonathan of his right to remain silent. In accordance with Russian procedure, Vasilyuk advised Jonathan that he had a right to remain silent at any stage of the proceedings. Jonathan nodded his head and began again.

"Members of the jury, as you know, my name is Jonathan Haynes." Jonathan's voice was soft, too soft. Chávez doubted the jury could hear him. Then he stopped as if he was unable to speak further. The jurors first looked at him, then looked down, apparently not sure what would come next.

Katya moved in her chair. Jonathan's eyes met hers, and he started again. "I did not rape and murder Olga

Sergova. I met Olga last summer when I was jogging in Gagarin Park. Our relationship developed slowly. We became friends, and eventually, I think we fell in love. I loved Olga, and I believe she loved me. My cell phone, which Investigator Masterkov took from me at the airport, would show that Olga and I began exchanging phone calls in July last summer."

"The last night before I left for home, we had dinner, talked, and danced. At her apartment, we made love. I left Olga's apartment about two a.m. and took a cab back to the Sapporo Hotel where I was staying. She was alive when I left her apartment—I loved Olga—I would never have hurt her in any way."

Jonathan continued to stand at the podium, but no words came out of his mouth. Instead, tears ran down his cheeks. Chávez started toward Jonathan. Katya got there first. She put her arm around Jonathan and directed him back to the cage. The guards remained motionless.

As the cage door clanged shut, Chávez walked from his place by the cage to the podium. He was not accustomed to using a podium during a trial. In front of a jury Chávez liked to move about the courtroom. He found the podium confining, both physically and mentally. He would start at the podium but move when he felt the need, assuming Judge Vasilyuk did not restrict him to the podium.

It was now up to Chávez to begin to provide the jury with reasons to doubt Barbatov's claims that Jonathan had raped and murdered Olga Sergova.

Chávez liked Barbatov's phrase "Citizens of the jury." He decided to begin that way. However, one last extraneous thought overtook him—"Please God, give me the strength to think like an American lawyer, but speak like a Russian."

Chávez began. "Citizens of the jury, I want to thank you on behalf of Jonathan Haynes for honoring us as jurors in this case. We know it is a sacrifice to be away from your jobs and your normal life. We all are here in this courtroom seeking justice. Ultimately, it will be up to each of you to provide that justice. Justice for the great country of Russia and justice for Jonathan Haynes."

Chávez paused and tried to make eye contact with the jurors. Then he continued. "Sometime after Jonathan left Olga Sergova's apartment, an intruder or intruders entered her apartment and strangled her. We may not be able to identify the actual murderer or murderers during this trial. However, at the end of the case, the evidence will leave you with more than a reasonable doubt about the identity of Olga Sergova's killer."

Chávez provided the details of Jonathan and Olga's six-month relationship and the physical evidence Chávez deemed inconsistent with Jonathan's guilt or which pointed to another killer. In particular, he emphasized three main points. First, Olga Sergova's clothes were folded neatly near her bed—evidence that she had voluntarily removed them and voluntarily gone to bed with Jonathan—contrary to the violent sexual assault that Barbatov claimed had preceded Sergova's death. Second, two unidentified fingerprints were found on the destroyed laptop computer, evidence that someone other than Olga Sergova had touched the laptop, likely the person who had destroyed the hard drive. That was evidence that someone else had been in the apartment and had a reason to be there. Chávez also noted that, in addition to the destroyed laptop, the desk and dresser drawers had been pulled out, and, in some cases, the drawer and its contents were on the floor. Again, evidence consistent with an unwanted intruder who was looking for something. Third, Chávez pointed out that Sergova had a cell phone and that the cell phone was also missing, further evidence that someone entered her apartment with a motive that went beyond just murdering her. The intruder had, for some reason, destroyed or removed things capable of storing information.

Chávez paused again, then he said, "Remember, Ms. Sergova was an investigative reporter. She likely stored investigative information on her computer and perhaps on her cell phone. In her job she had made enemies. Sergova's job as an investigative reporter and the facts I have just described is evidence indicating a motive for someone other than Jonathan Haynes to murder Sergova."

Finally, Chávez addressed Jonathan's alleged confession. He told the jury that Jonathan's confession should be viewed with skepticism. Chávez explained that Masterkov had written out the statement and Jonathan was so scared, fatigued, and disoriented that he did not know what he was signing.

Chávez ended by asking the jury to listen closely to the evidence, but to wait until they had heard all the evidence in the case before making a decision.

What Chávez did not mention, however, was anything about Sergei Egorov or the investigation that Kurilova had alluded to in her initial statement to Masterkov. First, he hoped that Barbatov would somehow alert the jury to the investigation when Masterkov's initial interview with Kurilova was put before the jury. Second, Chávez simply had no idea whether any of that evidence would get to the jury. One of the worst mistakes a criminal defense lawyer could make in an American courtroom was to promise the jury that certain evidence would be produced and then not deliver on that promise.

Chávez could tell that the jurors were paying close attention to him, which at that point was about as much as he could hope for.

Judge Vasilyuk now signaled that it was Barbatov's turn to begin presenting his evidence. Katya had painstakingly explained to Chávez that in a Russian criminal case, the prosecutor initially presented his or her case to the jury by reading to the jury the experts' reports from the investigative file and calling some important witnesses. That was another vestige of the old Soviet inquisitorial system still present in the new Russian adversarial system of justice.

Barbatov walked to the podium, opened the investigative file and began to read. Just as he had outlined in his opening statement, Barbatov methodically read Masterkov's reports along with the autopsy and fingerprint reports. It took Barbatov the remainder of that day and all of the next to read the reports to the jury. At the end, Barbatov read the confession slowly, looking up at the jury after each sentence, then at Jonathan in the cage.

As soon as Barbatov read the last sentence in Masterkov's report detailing Jonathan's confession, he announced, "I have no need of putting on any oral testimony, the evidence in the investigative file is clearly sufficient to prove that the defendant raped and murdered Olga Sergova."

Chávez had learned that, in the Soviet days, this would have been it. The defense attorney would have done nothing but urge his or her client to accept the evidence in the investigative file and then confess in open court. Things were supposed to be different now, though Chávez was not sure much had changed. When they returned to court on Monday, it would now be up to Chávez to demonstrate that Russia's so-called adversarial system could work on behalf of a criminal defendant.

CHAPTER

24

Masterkov slowly made his way down the snow-covered embankment. A trapper checking his trap lines had discovered the body face-down on the ice covering the river outside the small village north of the city. One of the *militsiya* that regularly patrolled the area had arrived first and had done an initial check for identification. Masterkov had received the radio message in route; no identification papers could be located on the dead man.

Masterkov reached the bottom of the embankment and stepped cautiously onto the river ice. Although the face of the dead man was frozen solid and distorted in death, Masterkov easily recognized the distinctive birthmark on the left side of the face and the hawklike nose. Masterkov was sure that Popov would confirm, through fingerprints, that the dead man was Sergei Egorov.

Other than the bullet hole behind the left ear, there were no obvious signs of trauma to the body. The bullet hole behind the left ear was significant, however. The location was consistent with a mafia-administered "control shot." Nearly all the murdered journalists throughout Russia had been administered a "control shot." As he looked around the immediate area, Masterkov concluded that it was unlikely that the criminalists would find much in the way of trace evidence at the scene. Six inches of snow in the last few hours had likely obliterated any tracks or other evidence of a struggle. In any event, Egorov could have been killed anywhere and the body only dumped at that location.

Masterkov flipped open his cell phone intending to request that a criminalist meet him in the village, where they would examine Egorov's apartment. He flipped the phone shut without punching in the numbers. He wanted to search the apartment one more time by himself. The first time he had been in the apartment, he had been in too much of a hurry. This time he would be more thorough. Dudinov and Chávez had been with Egorov in the apartment just days before. The official search requiring the presence of at least two lay witnesses could come later.

The apartment was trashed. It appeared that whoever killed Egorov had started the process in the apartment. Although he was not sure what he was searching for, Masterkov looked at and underneath the items overturned and strewn about the apartment. Everyone in Russia had a cell phone, yet there was none in the apartment. Inside a makeshift closet, Masterkov saw an army-type duffel bag, its apparent contents scattered about the floor. Masterkov turned the duffel bag inside out and pressed his hands firmly to the canvas. Eventually he felt something inside a small zipped pocket, deep in the interior of the bag.

Methodically he slipped a small photo from the concealed pocket. It was Olga eating at a restaurant and working on her laptop. For the first time in weeks he felt the rush of the raw sickening emotions that he had experienced when he had first seen Olga's beautiful but lifeless body laying across her bed. Olga's address was printed on the back of the photo.

CHAPTER

25

Chávez had spent the weekend reviewing, again and again, the fingerprint analysis and the autopsy of Sergova's body. Although the identification of Jonathan's fingerprint on the wine glass was accurate, and the autopsy findings competent, Chávez thought he could score some points with the jury if he could get Popov and Dr. Mitrokhin on the witness stand.

Judge Vasilyuk entered the courtroom promptly at nine, announcing as he entered, "Mr. Chávez and Mr. Barbatov, let's discuss Mr. Chávez's motion to examine Mr. Popov, Dr. Mitrokhin, Ms. Kurilova, and Mr. Egorov in front of the jury."

Barbatov started immediately. "Your Honor, you know our position on this. There is nothing to be gained from any of this. Every important fact that these witnesses have to say is in the investigative file. I am sure our citizen jurors are restless already. Nothing in our law requires you to permit this kind of American circus in our court-room."

Chávez attempted to read Vasilyuk's thoughts as Barbatov droned on about what an outrage it would be to have live testimony in a Russian courtroom. Eventually, Vasilyuk appeared to tire of Barbatov's harangue and turned in Chávez's direction.

"Your Honor, thank you. I disagree with just about everything Mr. Barbatov has said. I don't need to remind the court that the Russian Constitution states that criminal proceedings shall be conducted under the adversarial model and that the prosecution and defense shall be considered equal in court. The wise Russian scholars, judges, and lawyers who drafted the 1993 Constitution and the voters throughout Russia who approved it contemplated that some witnesses would be examined in front of the jury. As my motion papers indicate, there are a few issues that I wish to address with each of these witnesses that bear on the completeness of the investigation and cast doubt on the charge against my client. How can that be a bad thing? It won't take very long."

"Mr. Barbatov, are these witnesses available should I rule in favor of Mr. Chávez?"

Barbatov snapped back immediately, "Of course not. I never contemplated that you would agree to Mr. Chávez's outrageous requests."

"That will be enough, Mr. Barbatov," Judge Vasilyuk said firmly, looking in the direction of the foreign press, "Just answer my questions. Do you have the witnesses present, and, if not, how soon can you have the bailiffs' service get them here?"

"I don't know. Inspector Popov and Dr. Mitrokhin have important investigative duties and busy schedules. We know nothing of the Kurilova woman or this Egorov.

Obviously, Kurilova is a private citizen. She could be anywhere," Barbatov shot back.

Then, with a smirk, Barbatov finished, "In any event, I would need to meet with Prokuror General Karpov before I can agree to any order you may think you have the power to enter."

Chávez could hardly believe his ears. Prosecutors in America often disagreed with a judge's ruling. But in the main, they were respectful of the role of the court. Outright defiance was rare. Old habits from the Soviet period when the prosecutor had all the power and judges were mere functionaries were hard to break. However, before Chávez could respond, Judge Vasilyuk thundered back.

"Investigator Masterkov, come to the witness podium. I hereby order you to have the bailiffs' service bring Inspector Popov and Dr. Mitrokhin to the courtroom immediately. The investigative file shows that Ms. Kurilova works for *Sovietsky Sakhalin*. Have them also pick her up. Mr. Chávez's motion does not explain what this Mr. Egorov has to do with this case. Mr. Chávez, I intend to deny your motion to examine Mr. Egorov for two reasons. I don't see in the investigative file that you ever informed Investigator Masterkov about this citizen nor that you requested that Masterkov interview the witness. You were required to do that under our criminal procedure code. Unless you have more specific information you care to share with us in court today, your motion and written representation regarding the need for citizen Egorov is legally insufficient."

Just as Chávez started to explain the need for Egorov's testimony, Masterkov interrupted. "Your Honor,

I am afraid the Egorov matter is a moot point. That man is dead."

Judge Vasilyuk had no visual or oral response to Masterkov's announcement. Instead, he said, "We will resume at one o'clock. Mr. Barbotov, I expect you to have the witnesses here."

Before Chávez could respond to anything, Judge Vasilyuk was up and headed for the door to his chambers. Chávez had been warned by Judge Vasilyuk not to talk to the press. Although Judge Vasilyuk had never said exactly what the penalty would be if Chávez defied Vasilyuk's gag order, he was certain he did not want to find out. Chávez had intended that the argument he had prepared to attempt to convince Judge Vasilyuk to permit him to question Egorov in front of the jury would also alert the foreign press to the fact that Egorov had been solicited to murder Olga Sergova. That plan had now gone awry.

CHAPTER

26

Masterkov's cell phone rang within minutes after he left the courtroom. Not surprisingly, he was summoned immediately to Karpov's office. Barbatov was already there when Masterkov entered.

"Alexander, do you know anything more about the Kurilova woman?" Karpov barked as Masterkov sat down.

"General Karpov, not long after Sergova's murder, I attempted a routine follow-up interview with Ms. Kurilova. She was no longer employed at the newspaper. She could not be located at her apartment."

"What do you mean, Alexander? Is she still living in her apartment here in Yuzhno or not?"

Masterkov knew he was at a crossroads. Kurilova had worked closely with Olga. He suspected that she knew a great deal about the investigation that Olga was working on when she was murdered. Yet, she had told him hardly anything, only that it had something to do with the oil and gas companies and pipeline construction. She claimed that she had left the newspaper and left Yuzhno simply because she wanted to do something else, not because she was afraid that someone other than

Jonathan Haynes had murdered Olga and had the same thing in mind for her.

"I just mean that she was not in her apartment on the two occasions that I went there." Then, attempting to appear completely disinterested and as unengaged as possible, Masterkov lied. "General, there is nothing in the initial statement that I took from her in the car and had her sign the next day that would be of assistance to our case. So I did nothing further."

"What about Dudinov, is he looking for her?" Karpov asked firmly.

Again, Masterkov instantaneously weighed the effect of different responses. "Perhaps, but so far I have received no information that he has found her. My agents are watching him closely."

At that, Karpov seemed to tire of the meeting. His face was cast in weariness, and, Masterkov thought for the first time, uncertainty. Surprisingly, Karpov had said nothing about Masterkov's recent report on Egorov's murder.

"Very well, Alexander. Bring Popov and Dr. Mitrokhin to the courtroom. Andre, tell Judge Vasilyuk we have had no contact with Kurilova, and we can't begin looking for her now."

As soon as the meeting with Karpov ended, Masterkov called Popov and Dr. Mitrokhin and ordered them to the courtroom. Each man expressed displeasure. Masterkov, however, perceived that each man simply resented the interruption from their normal routine, not that they were worried about anything that Chávez might have waiting for them in the courtroom. Masterkov believed that attitude was mistaken. Popov and Mitrokhin had no real experience in court and had never faced a skilled examiner like Chávez.

Masterkov was distracted by a number of thoughts and questions as he made his way back to the courthouse. Why was Karpov so preoccupied with Kurilova? She could add nothing to the Prokuror's case. Barbatov could report that she had left the newspaper and could not be located at her apartment. Vasilyuk would have to be satisfied with that answer.

The directional bug was no longer transmitting. Either Dudinov had found it and destroyed it, or the bug was inoperable for some other reason. Masterkov had no idea whether Dudinov had located Kurilova. Chávez had said nothing in court to let on either way.

And Karpov had said nothing about Masterkov's short report announcing the discovery of Egorov's body. Only the official search of Egorov's apartment was mentioned in the short report. Nothing of evidentiary significance had been found. Olga's photo with her address on the back remained hidden in Masterkov's spacious apartment, as was the Detention Center order that Masterkov had found in Egorov's apartment. That order confirmed Egorov's confinement and that Egorov could not have been Olga's killer. The evidence against Haynes remained rock solid. He could not, however, erase from his mind that many of the contract murders he had investigated in the past revealed that there had been multiple solicitations before the murder was actually carried out.

In any event, the adversarial system, as mandated in the Constitution, was about to make an appearance on the Island of Sakhalin in the form of Chávez's in-court examination of Popov and Mitrokhin. Each time Masterkov contemplated the unusual decisions being made by Judge Vasilyuk and Karpov he was more convinced that the Kremlin was in control of both the court and Karpov. Apparently, Vasilyuk and Karpov really had no choice.

CHAPTER

27

As soon as he left the courtroom, Chávez dialed Dudinov's cell number. It went to voicemail. However, seconds later, Chávez's cell phone rang identifying Dudinov as the caller.

"Yes, Ivan." Chávez began in Russian.

"Peter, I got your message, Masterkov was telling the truth. Egorov is dead. It appears to be a hit. He was found frozen in river ice. I think I know where to find Kurilova."

Dudinov clicked off before Chávez could respond.

There was no time to think about Egorov's murder. Chávez would demand a copy of Masterkov's report to see if there was something in it that might prove to be helpful. Katya had previously explained that under Russian law the defense could request that Masterkov interview Egorov. However, Chávez had rejected that idea preferring to file the motion requesting that he be allowed to call Egorov as a witness in the defense case. Chávez had calculated that his in-court statements about Egorov's proposed testimony in front of the foreign press would pressure Vasilyuk or whoever was calling the shots to permit Egorov's testimony in front of the jury. That now appeared to have been a serious mistake. However, just like any other trial, Chávez had to put that mistake aside and concentrate on Popov and Dr. Mitrokhin.

Chávez's eyes followed Popov as he made his way to the witness podium. Popov was short and stocky, with a round face. Although he was technically part of law enforcement, he did not wear a uniform. Instead, he was dressed in a well-fitting black sport coat, pressed blue shirt and gray slacks. Chávez wondered if Popov might have purchased the sport coat in America or perhaps Italy, certainly not in Russia.

With Popov leaning against the witness podium, Chávez began his examination by asking about the techniques used to preserve the fingerprints in Sergova's apartment. Popov gave concise answers to each of the questions. Chávez was confident that Popov would acknowledge the two unidentified fingerprints on Sergova's laptop computer but would also tell the jury that there were almost always unidentified prints at any crime scene. However, before eliciting those obvious answers, Chávez decided to see if he might first put Popov a bit on the defensive.

"Mr. Popov, do you feel that you did a thorough examination of the apartment for latent prints?"

"Yes," Popov replied without elaboration.

"Is it possible to detect latent prints on different surfaces, such as glass, steel, wood, leather, skin, cloth?"

"Yes, it is possible to detect prints on each of the surfaces you mentioned. It all depends on the circumstances."

"Mr. Popov, did you examine for latent prints on cloth material in this case?" "Yes, we examined the bedding and various clothing articles. There were no other useable prints."

Although there logically was another question to follow immediately, Chávez was not yet ready to ask that question. "Thank you, Mr. Popov. Let me ask you about the latent prints that were found on the wine glasses on the drain board in the apartment. Can you tell us, were those prints easily detectible?"

"Yes, prints on a smooth surface like glass are easy to detect. And, as I said in my report, your client's fingerprint was perfectly preserved."

"Thank you. Are prints on other less smooth surfaces more difficult to recover?" Chávez continued.

"Yes."

"Mr. Popov, let's discuss the two unidentified fingerprints on the laptop computer. Were they easily detectible?"

"Yes, again, the metal surface is smooth, similar to the glass surface."

"Regarding the laptop, is there anything notable about the latent prints discovered on the laptop?"

Popov hesitated. "I am not sure I understand the nature of your question."

"In your report, you indicate that these prints were particularly clear, am I right about that?"

Popov looked closely at his report, glanced over at Barbatov, and then looked plaintively at Judge Vasilyuk, "Yes, the prints were unusually clear."

Chávez thought Popov had given an honest answer, so he decided to try a leading question because, even if Barbatov objected, the jury would get the idea. "Would you agree, Mr. Popov, that the unidentified prints on the laptop could have been placed there at the same time as the prints on the wine glasses?"

Barbatov jumped up immediately, "That question is improper."

Judge Vasilyuk agreed, "Again, Mr. Chávez, your questions must be open-ended. We have covered this before."

Chávez smiled. "Thank you, Your Honor. I will rephrase the question. Mr. Popov, can you determine the age of a fingerprint?"

"Other than the particular circumstances of a case, there is no scientific way to determine that."

"So the prints on the laptop could have been made on the same evening."

"Yes, of course."

Chávez glanced at the jury and then continued. "Would you agree that the reason that the prints on the laptop were so clear is that the person who left those prints could have been perspiring profusely, say from physical exertion, so much so, that an unusual amount of perspiration was on the person's fingertips?"

The question was clearly objectionable because it was compound, containing two propositions—perspiration and physical exertion—to which the witness was asked to agree.

Barbatov said nothing.

"Yes, you are correct. Either perspiration or some oily substance was present on the person's fingertips."

Instantly Chávez asked, "In that kind of situation, is there a good chance of recovering a latent print from a person's skin?"

Popov's lower lip seemed noticeably to twitch. He looked over at Barbatov. Barbatov seemed not to sense danger. "It depends," Popov answered cautiously.

"Mr. Popov, did you or any of your technicians attempt to recover latent prints from Ms. Sergova's body?"

Popov looked over at Barbatov.

"Objection! Again, Mr. Chávez seeks to violate our rules to suit his own purposes." Barbatov shouted.

Chávez responded quickly. "It's not leading if that's the objection."

Vasilyuk agreed. "Overruled, Mr. Barbatov."

"Mr. Popov, do you understand my question?" Chávez forcefully inquired.

"Yes, Mr. Chávez, I understand. There was no effort to recover latent prints from the body. We are reluctant to do so for fear of contaminating other trace evidence that the criminalists or the pathologist might recover from the body."

It was a reasonable answer, but not a complete one. Only another witness to come later could supply a complete answer.

"Nevertheless, Mr. Popov, you could have examined Ms. Sergova's neck for fingerprints."

"Yes, it is possible, but as I explained it would risk contamination of other trace evidence. There is a choice to be made in these circumstances," Popov responded uncomfortably.

Out of the corner of his eye Chávez could see a number of jurors leaning forward in their chairs. They were interested, engaged in the process.

"Again, Mr. Popov, assume a person is either sweating profusely or has a substance like oil on their fingertips. In that situation, is there a good chance of recovering a latent print from a cloth surface?"

"There can be, yes."

"Did you examine Ms. Sergova's clothes?"

"Yes."

"Do you recall that certain clothing items were found folded neatly on the chair near Sergova's bed?"

"Yes," Popov replied.

Chávez quickly followed up, "And there were no useable prints found on those clothes?"

Popov nodded his head and responded, "Yes."

As soon as Popov said yes, Chávez asked, "Can you lift prints from silk?"

"Yes."

"Would a latent print be easy to detect on silk if the person was sweating profusely or had an oily substance on their fingertips?"

"Yes, that is possible."

"Mr. Popov, does your report, the one that Mr. Barbatov read to our jurors, reflect everything you examined in the case and everything you did in the case?"

Popov paused and again looked at Barbatov. It was an unfair question. He was not in the courtroom when Barbatov read the report to the jury. Nevertheless, Barbatov looked away.

"Yes, I believe my report is complete."

Chávez had spent hours studying the reports in the investigative file. As best he could determine, Sergova's nightshirt and panties had disappeared somewhere

190

between Sergova's apartment and Popov's fingerprint lab. They were never transported to Popov's lab and were mentioned only in the first report of the inventory of items taken from Sergova's apartment.

"Mr. Popov, you were not sent a nightshirt and a pair of women's silk underwear to be examined?"

Barbatov's head jerked straight up. Popov looked for help, first to Barbatov, then to Judge Vasilyuk. None was forthcoming.

Barbatov finally stood up. "Your Honor, I object to this type of questioning. It really has nothing to do with the case. Perhaps there has been a mistake—perhaps evidence has been mislaid. Nevertheless, it has no effect on this case."

Before Vasilyuk could say anything, Chávez inserted, "Mr. Popov, a complete investigation would have included an examination of the nightshirt and panties. The unidentified fingerprints on the laptop could have matched a fingerprint on the nightshirt or the missing silk panties or, for that matter, a fingerprint on Ms. Sergova's neck?"

Both Vasilyuk and Barbatov were raising their voices.

"Don't answer, improper question," reverberated around the courtroom. Chávez looked at the jury, his eyes asking them, "Do you get the point?"

Chávez then turned away and returned to his seat near the cage. As he did, looking at the jury, he announced, "Your witness, Mr. Barbatov."

Barbatov asked Popov the usual questions about unidentified prints. Popov gave the usual responses.

There were always unidentified prints at a crime scene; it was routine. Barbatov said nothing about the missing nightshirt or silk panties or the potential for fingerprints on Sergova's neck.

Popov seemed a bit shorter as he hurried from the witness stand. Chávez and Katya made eye contact. Chávez detected a very faint smile crease Katya's face. Jonathan seemed to sit a little straighter. However, there would be no recess. Dr. Mitrokhin was next.

Like he did with Popov, Chávez studied Dr. Mitrokhin closely as he made his way to the witness podium. Dr. Mitrokhin's brown hair was combed straight back. However, it was his rimless eyeglasses and brown goatee that truly evoked the appearance of the Marxist revolutionary Leon Trotsky.

"Dr. Mitrokhin, I understand that you have been the medical examiner for the Sakhalin region for twelve years." Although not really a question, Mitrokhin nodded his head affirmatively and answered, "Yes."

"Dr. Mitrokhin, as a medical examiner, how often have you concluded that a murder victim was also sexually assaulted?"

Mitrokhin hesitated, as any witness might with such an open-ended question. Getting no clarification from Barbatov or Judge Vasilyuk, Mitrokhin answered, "I don't know really, but perhaps a hundred, counting my medical training and all the time I have been a pathologist."

"Was Sergova's body clothed?"

Mitrokhin appeared to be looking at his notes. The jury looked quizzically at Mitrokhin.

"The body was not clothed."

"Was the body transported in a special body bag?"

"Ah, yes it was," Mitrokhin answered haltingly.

"Did you retain the body bag used to transport the body?"

Chávez noticed that slight beads of sweat begin to appear at Mitrokhin's temples.

"No, we incinerate the bags once the body is removed." That was the answer Chávez had hoped for. No further searching for or testing of the bag was possible. "Is the bag checked for trace evidence before it is burned?"

"I don't understand your question."

"Did you or someone else look for loose hair, fiber, or anything that might have adhered to the body but come off in transport to your facility?"

"I don't recall," was all Mitrokhin could say in an almost inaudible voice.

Chávez had a choice. He could press further, or argue later to the jury that there was no indication the body bag had been examined. The investigation was sloppy. He chose the latter course.

"Did you ever see any silk panties as part of the evidence in this case?"

"No."

Chávez could see Mitrokhin's body seem to relax, as if to say the worst is over, I am back on firm ground. Chávez would now demonstrate that that assumption was a mistake.

"Dr. Mitrokhin, tell the jury about your observations regarding the victim's death and the cause of her death."

"The victim was manually strangled," Mitrokhin answered. "The force was so great it broke her hyoid bone, which is common among manual strangulation victims."

"Dr. Mitrokhin, I have some photos I want you to look at."

"Objection, what photos?" Barbatov exclaimed.

"The photos Dr. Mitrokhin took of the victim's neck area. They are in the investigative file. You showed them to the jury as you read Dr. Mitrokhin's report to the jury," Chávez answered.

"Let me see them," Judge Vasilyuk demanded.

Chávez handed Vasilyuk the two photos. "Compare them, Your Honor. They are copies of what you have in your file. I could just use the ones in your file if you like."

Chávez was shocked that Vasilyuk was comparing the photos. For a moment Chávez reflected on where he was. In America, almost no one would think that a lawyer would doctor a photo, particularly when the opponent had the original. That was not so in Russia. Corruption permeated all aspects of Russian life, including the court-room. In fact, in Russia, lawyers had to present their iden-tification to judges in court to prove who they were before they could start a case. Vasilyuk looked at the pho-tos, assuring himself they were identical.

"Yes, Mr. Chávez, these photos are identical. You may proceed."

Chávez had the photos handed to Dr. Mitrokhin. "Do you recognize the photos, which I have asked to be identified as separate defense exhibits?"

"Yes."

"Did you take the photographs?"

"Yes."

"Using both photos, do you see some discoloration on the front of the victim's neck and on the back of the victim's neck?"

"Yes."

"Would you agree that the discoloration indicates bruising that occurred by the force of the strangulation?"

Barbatov said nothing about the leading nature of the question.

"Yes, the pressure or force broke blood vessels, causing the discoloration."

"Could the discoloration on the front and back represent pressure points, say the tips of the perpetrator's thumbs and forefingers?"

"It is possible, but I cannot be positive," Mitrokhin asserted. He then seemed to stand more erect, apparently certain he had given a competent, professional answer to the question.

"What is the distance between the pressure points on the front of her neck and the one on the back?"

Barbatov was on his feet objecting loudly.

Judge Vasilyuk held up his hand. "Mr. Barbatov, the question was not objectionable."

Judge Vasilyuk looked at Mitrokhin. "Answer the question, Dr. Mitrokhin."

"I don't know, I did not make any such measurement."

"Would you agree any measurement of the distance of the points on the neck, inconsistent with the measurement of Mr. Haynes' hands is evidence my client did not strangle Sergova?"

Barbatov objected loudly.

Chávez changed course. "Dr. Mitrokhin, did you request that Sergova's neck be examined for latent fingerprints?"

Mitrokhin was now so bewildered that he made no attempt to answer. He slumped noticeably at the witness podium. Chávez answered for him. "No, you failed to request an examination for latent fingerprints on the neck."

There was only one more question to ask. "Dr. Mitrokhin, you indicated that you observed some redness, discoloration, and apparent trauma to Sergova's vagina." Again, it was not a question. Nevertheless, Mitrokhin, apparently weary of the intellectual combat, never raised his eyes to meet Chávez's. Instead, he simply nodded his head affirmatively.

"In Ms. Sergova's case there was no tearing or other disruption of the vagina, correct?" Chávez inquired.

Again, without looking at the jury or at Chávez, Mitrokhin nodded his agreement with Chávez's observation.

"Thank you. Can the redness you observed just as likely be the result of vigorous consensual sexual intercourse, particularly a woman who has not been having sexual intercourse regularly?"

Perhaps if it were not nearly five o'clock, perhaps if Barbatov and Mitrokhin were not shaken from the earlier questions, perhaps Barbatov would have objected to the question. Perhaps Mitrokhin would have given a better answer. Perhaps. Instead, Mitrokhin said, "Yes, that could be."

"Thank you," Chávez said, "I have no further questions."

Barbatov had no questions for the puzzled Dr. Mitrokhin.

CHAPTER

28

Ty, che, blyad ("What the fuck"). The words kept thundering in Masterkov's head. The ripped nightshirt and a ripped pair of panties were near the bed when he had first entered Olga's bedroom. The criminalists had put each item in a separate evidence bag.

He was in the lounge at the Eurasia Hotel to meet someone. But first he needed to look at the reports prepared by the criminalists. A cognac arrived at the out-of-the-way booth just as Masterkov opened his laptop. Quickly he brought up on his laptop the criminalists' reports listing the evidence seized in the bedroom.

Yes. The nightshirt and panties were listed on the initial report. However, the report listing the items sent from fingerprint examination and other scientific analysis did not include either the nightshirt or panties.

Masterkov shook his head slightly and downed the cognac. First, Haynes' cell phone had disappeared from the evidence locker, and now it appeared that Olga's panties and nightshirt had never made it from her apartment to the forensic laboratory. Unfortunately, problems in the transfer of evidence from one agency to another were common. He was sure the evidence would never be located, and no one in the lab would admit responsibility. In the end, it was his fault. He should have personally supervised every aspect of the case, including the transfer of the physical evidence to the forensic laboratory. The cell phone, however, was a different issue. Someone had taken the cell phone; it was not simply lost like the panties and nightshirt.

What really bothered Masterkov, however, was how Chávez had used the lost evidence to his advantage in the courtroom. Hell, if there were fingerprints on the panties or nightshirt they could have been Haynes' prints. Yet Chávez made it appear to the jury that somehow the lost evidence would have proved the killer was not Haynes— which seemed to Masterkov to be mostly bullshit.

A second cognac arrived just as his cousin on his mother's side, Nadezhda, slipped into a seat across from him. As usual her hair was dyed jet-black and her face was heavily made up, giving her the appearance of gypsy fortuneteller, or a madam, the latter being accurate. Nadezhda wasted little time with preliminaries.

"Sasha, thank you for coming over. I know you are very busy. I think I made a mistake, and I think I need to talk to you about it. It's about the Haynes case. I should have told you about this earlier. I know you are familiar with that man Ivan Dudinov."

"Yes, what about Dudinov?" Masterkov replied, trying not to show his concern for what he was now sure would be another dose of bad news.

"Well, you know that I have known Dudinov for a few years. Once he took care of a problem that one of my girls had with one of the American oil workers."

"Yes, I remember," Masterkov replied evenly.

"Yes, well, Dudinov stopped by one night, and we were talking. It was just a conversation over a drink. He was inquiring about a guy who comes in here who owed him some money. Anyway, uh, I told him about one of my girls, Tatiana. It really wasn't much, just that she thought that one of her customers, a Georgian, had a small photo of that Sergova woman the black guy is supposed to have murdered. Actually, I think that when she told me, I remembered the guy. He was tall, a shaved head. I remember thinking that I had not seen him before and that he might be mafia, perhaps from St. Petersburg or Moscow."

The words *ty, che, blyad* were again on the tip of Masterkov's tongue. Again, however, he replied evenly, "You actually told this to Dudinov?"

"Uh yeah. Alexander, I really had no idea it was important or that Dudinov would somehow become involved in the case. It was before you arrested the black guy. I was just making conversation, really. I am sorry, but I just wanted you to know about this."

"Okay, cousin, but why are you telling me this now? Has something else occurred?"

"Ah, yes, Alexander. That is why I called. Dudinov came back here a couple of days ago. He wants to find Tatiana. He wanted to know everything I could tell him about where she might be. Alexander, I told him everything I knew. I told him that I thought she had gone to Thailand, at least for the winter." Then she paused, her dark expressive eyes growing wider, and she repeated, "I am sure that he is looking for her. He scares me. You know Dudinov is a kind of dangerous man."

Although his cousin seemed to be looking for reassurance that nothing bad would come of the whole thing, Masterkov could not satisfy that need. "Cousin, you are right to tell me. Do you think you gave Dudinov enough information to find this Tatiana?"

"I don't know. I am scared about this," she replied.

Masterkov, now anticipating further unforeseen developments, said, "Okay, Nadezhda, now I need you to tell me everything you know about Tatiana, and I hope it is more than you told Dudinov. Start first by telling me everything this Tatiana told you about the guy and the photo. And anything else you might recall about that night independently of what this Tatiana told you. And what the hell is Tatiana's last name? Is she from here? Does she have parents on the island?"

CHAPTER

29

A blizzard had struck the city on Monday evening just as Chávez had wrapped up his cross-examination of Dr. Mitrokhin. The storm, which the Russians called a cyclone, had continued relentlessly for the rest of the week. Because a number of the jurors could not reach the courthouse Judge Vasilyuk had no choice but to postpone everything until the following Monday. Chávez had used the four-day respite to catch up on things in the U.S. The telephone conversations with the Oregon senators, particularly with Senator Garlock, did not go well. They were increasingly concerned about his activities in Russia. Garlock even asked him if he had given any thought to withdrawing from the confirmation process. Each night during the week his dreams were a jumble of events from the past and the present leaving him unrefreshed each morning and filled with self-doubt and unrelenting anxiety. The problem was not that the trial would not end in time for Chávez to return to the United States for his confirmation hearing. Instead, the problem was the trial was going to end, and without some unforeseen event the trial was going to end badly. The thought that he would fail in Russia and doom his judgeship was never far from his conscious thoughts. What he actually hated about those thoughts was not just the anxiety it caused him, but that the thoughts were so self-centered and he thought so weak—at a time when he needed to be solely focused on the battle for Jonathan Haynes' life.

Now, seated at the desk in his hotel room early on Saturday morning, Chávez sipped his coffee and, for just a few minutes, permitted his mind to turn away from the case against Jonathan Haynes—this time toward his relationship with Katya—a relationship that he now believed transcended the Haynes' case. He and Katya had met for dinner every evening. The night before, Katya had invited Peter to her apartment for dinner. His physical and emotional attraction to her was real. He thought she felt the same way. That night as they said goodbye at her door, he had put his arms out to her, and Katya had come to him. She wrapped her arms around his neck and kissed him. The touch of her body and her soft lips excited him in a way he had not experienced since the first time he had kissed Claire and held her close to him. Although Katya's lips were responsive, she had not invited him to stay.

The ringing of his cell phone jarred Chávez from those new, sometimes pleasant, sometimes unsettling thoughts about Katya. It was Dudinov. "I have found Kurilova, I will pick up Katya and be there to pick you up in a couple of minutes."

Within minutes he and Katya were in Dudinov's Lexus headed over snow-covered roads to a remote area near the village of Tymovskoye.

Seconds after they entered the car, Dudinov began describing his difficulties in finding Kurilova and his almost fatal encounter with her father. However, as Dudinov explained in great detail, it turned out that Kurilova's father was also an Afghanistan veteran. Eventually, the veterans shared a shot of vodka, toasting their fallen comrades. As they cleared the city limits Dudinov described his interview with Kurilova.

"Masterkov has talked to her twice. Kurilova was surprised that he had found her in Tymovskoye. Masterkov did not tape or make notes of the second interview at her parents' cabin—at least not that she was aware of. He asked her a lot of questions about Sergova. Things like whether Sergova had ever mentioned your client and about the story Sergova was working on when she was murdered. He even asked her if she remembered Sergova's cell number. Of course she did. For reasons that will soon become clear to you, she told Masterkov nothing about what I am about to tell you."

Almost instantly, Chávez could tell from Dudinov's emotional and rapid speech that Dudinov thought Kurilova held some sort of key to the case. For the first time since he had arrived in Russia, Chávez sensed that he just might find a path to a successful defense for Jonathan. He made no outward response to Dudinov's first comments, eager for more.

"Kurilova did not know about Jonathan Haynes. She had never seen Sergova with him, nor had Sergova ever mentioned him to her. However, Kurilova thought that Sergova might have been seeing someone, but for some reason, she wasn't ready to talk about it."

Chávez asked, "How close was the relationship between Sergova and Kurilova?"

"They were close," Dudinov responded. "I have the feeling Sergova was something like an older sister. Kurilova looked up to her, wanted to follow in her footsteps as a journalist. She had worked with Sergova on a couple of in-depth investigative stories."

"Did she say what kind of stories?" Chávez interjected.

"About a year ago, Sergova did a series of articles about the head of some department of the Tax Ministry. The guy was receiving bribes from various businesses in return for special regulatory favors. As a result of those articles, Karpov's office eventually charged the man in criminal court. It was Masterkov who did the official investigation."

Chávez looked back at Katya, "I see, so Sergova actually was a good investigative reporter."

Dudinov did not respond to Chávez's observation but continued the story, one hand on the steering wheel, the other jabbing the air as he emphasized points of his report.

"About two months ago, before she was murdered, Sergova received an anonymous letter. The letter accused the Governor and the Prokuror General of receiving kickbacks from various contractors involved in laying the oil and natural gas pipelines for the energy projects off the northern coast to the southern tip of the island."

Chávez was stunned. "You mean the letter claimed that Karpov was involved in the kickbacks?"

"Yes, that's exactly who and what I mean," Dudinov replied instantly.

With his free hand Dudinov reached into the left breast pocket of his leather jacket and pulled out a piece of paper and handed it to Chávez.

"Here is a copy of the letter. Kurilova had saved a couple of copies."

It was handwritten, so Chávez had to go slowly to decipher the Cyrillic characters. Dudinov paraphrased as Chávez read. "Although the bidding was supposed to be competitive, certain contractors bidding on various aspects of the pipeline construction, to assure they were awarded the bid, paid the Governor and the Prokuror General through some phony consulting companies to rig the selection process through their influence with Rus-Energy."

"Chávez, I am sure you know that Rus-Energy is one of the Russian state-owned gas and oil companies and is a co-partner in each of the six Sakhalin energy projects. In some of these projects, Rus-Energy has a greater than fifty percent share; in others, it is smaller. Recently the Kremlin has been trying to renegotiate Rus-Energy's share to a majority position in each project. The Kremlin uses the environmental laws to harass the multinationals to get them to give up a percentage of their interest. But that's another matter."

Chávez nodded and returned to the letter.

Dudinov continued his paraphrase, shifting his eyes from the road to the letter and back.

"As you can see, the letter alleges that four of the contractors on the pipeline project paid a total of $2 million U.S. for help in securing the contracts. The contracts total more than $800 million."

As Dudinov concluded, Chávez realized that, apart from a plea that Sergova investigate the matter, there was not much more in the letter. "So, is there more from Kurilova?"

"Yes, some," Dudinov responded. "In November, Sergova started nosing around. She contacted the Governor's office requesting an interview. She was turned down. She did not contact Karpov, however. Next, she turned her attention to the pipeline contractors. It turns out none of them have their principal office in Sakhalin. One is located in Vladivostok, two are located in Khabarovsk, and one as far away as Krasnodar. Of course they denied it. She asked to see their books; they told her to go to hell.

"She also contacted representatives of Rus-Energy and Exxon. Exxon actually responded. They sent her a letter denying any wrongdoing. They claimed that those bids were awarded solely by Rus-Energy, and that as far as they knew the bids were awarded competitively and that there were many factors that went into the award process. No one from Rus-Energy responded to her."

"Does the letter from Exxon exist?" Chávez inquired.

"Perhaps, but Kurilova never saw it. Sergova only told her about it. Sergova kept her investigative notes on her laptop."

Dudinov continued, "Sergova then got another letter. Kurilova never saw it either. However, somehow the author of the letter and Sergova arranged a meeting.

According to Kurilova, Sergova secretly met with this guy two days before she was murdered. He told Sergova that Karpov had registered bogus consulting companies and had offshore accounts where he hid the money. Karpov transferred a share of the funds to the Governor. The man promised Sergova that he could produce the account records for the Governor. That, unfortunately, never happened. As I said, Kurilova has no idea who the guy is. Sergova told Kurilova that she thought the guy was some kind of computer hacker."

As Dudinov paused, Chávez interjected, "But aren't the contracts private ones? How could the Governor or the Prokuror General influence the contract awards?"

Katya answered immediately, "It's all about the environmental laws and regulations. The Prokuror General rates the contractors on environmental compliance on previous projects. A bad word from the Prokuror General, and you can kiss any contract good-bye. And, the Prokuror General or the Governor can shut these projects down in a heartbeat for alleged environmental violations. Any delay on the projects can cost the companies millions, even billions. And I assume Karpov knows many of the Rus-Energy executives personally. Karpov probably arranged other kickbacks from the contractors to Rus-Energy executives."

Chávez nodded and then asked Dudinov, "How solid is Kurilova? Do you think she will testify, and would she hold up in court if the judge would let me question her?"

Dudinov responded, "She's smart, but she's afraid of Karpov. However, there is one thing that I am sure of. She won't tell the Prokuror's office or Masterkov that she has talked with us. She thinks Masterkov is okay, but she thinks Karpov will kill her if he knows that she was privy to Sergova's investigation. She is very worried that Masterkov might tell Karpov where she is."

Chávez looked back at Katya. Her face was ashen. Chávez surmised that Katya was contemplating what a dangerous mess they were in. Likely she was envisioning him in open court, accusing the Governor and the Prokuror General of the Region of taking bribes—believing that if he did that, they both could end up in prison or dead.

"We don't have to tell Barbatov or Masterkov about this, do we?"

"It's not quite that simple," Katya responded. "Based on what Barbatov told Vasilyuk in court, Karpov likely does not know that Masterkov had found Kurilova. There is no official report of Masterkov's second interview with Kurilova. As Ivan said when we first met with him, Karpov and Masterkov are often not on the same page. In any event, Kurilova's statements to Masterkov at the apartment are in the investigative file. Barbatov already read that to the jury. Remember when we discussed what to do when we thought that Egorov could be a witness? At a minimum we have to give notice to Barbatov and tell Judge Vasilyuk that we have questions to ask Kurilova in front of the jury. Perhaps we can indicate vaguely that the questions we want to ask involve Kurilova's observations of the door, the apartment, and some other matters. You can be sure, Peter, that once you begin the questions regarding this subject, Barbatov will go wild. It is anyone's guess how Judge Vasilyuk will rule."

"That's what I thought," Chávez replied, wondering how a legal system could be so screwed up.

Sarcastically, Chávez added, "I doubt Judge Vasilyuk will compel the Governor or Karpov to court so I can question them about an anonymous letter accusing them of misusing their offices."

At Chávez's last comment, Dudinov and Katya looked at each other quizzically. Katya then responded, "Peter, I guess you didn't know. The Governor referred to in that letter—Alexei Bergovsky—is dead. Right before the New Year, Bergovsky and some other Sakhalin administration officials were on a helicopter up in Kamchatka. The helicopter crashed, and they were all killed. I guess most of the news about the crash and the funerals were out of the papers and television by the time you arrived on Sakhalin."

"I see." Secretly, Chávez thought, "Of course, this is Russia; always expect the unexpected."

They reached Tymovskoye in the fading winter light, taking a narrow snow-bound road leading east of the small village. Chávez calculated that they had gone about ten kilometers on the barely passable road when Dudinov suddenly stopped the car and pointed to a small cabin only partially visible from the road. A light flickered in one of the windows of the cabin.

They walked through the snow and were within a short distance of the dwelling when a man, armed with a rifle, stepped from behind a tree directly into their path. Chávez hoped that it was Kurilova's father. Apparently recognizing Dudinov, the man instantly lowered his rifle as Dudinov identified Chávez and Katya to Mr. Kurilov. In response Kurilov directed them into the cabin.

Chávez had the sense he was entering a Russian fairy tale. The cabin was built of a combination of milled lumber and rough-hewn logs. The floor was made of pine, seemingly polished smooth by years of wear. Oil lamps provided the cabin's only light. A large woodstove heated the main room. Two chairs and a small sofa covered with a bearskin were arranged near the woodstove. Mrs. Kurilova, a plump woman in her mid-fifties with a round, smiling face, immediately offered hot tea, which Peter and Katya gladly accepted.

As he took his first sip of the honey-flavored Russian tea, Chávez concluded that he had indeed entered a Tolstoy novel. Gathered in the cabin were remnants of the old Russia, people like the Kurilovs still connected to the earth and having a spiritual allegiance to *Rodina*, the image of Mother Russia. Dudinov, Katya, and the Kurilov's daughter, Natalia, embodied modern Russia and its conflicting set of post-Soviet and western ideals.

Just after the warm cup of tea was placed in his hands, Chávez observed Natalia Kurilova move out of the shadows to a place near the woodstove. She was a petite young woman, about five foot five with blonde hair cut short, almost boy-like, giving her an elfin-like appearance. There was no outward sign that she was in any way nervous or apprehensive about the meeting—a good sign if Chávez could convince Judge Vasilyuk to let him put Natalia Kurilova on the stand in front of the jury.

Just as they had agreed in the car, Katya began the conversation. "Natalia, thank you so much for speaking with us. What you have to say to us could prove to be very important. Please trust me; a man's life likely depends on the information you can provide us."

Natalia looked at her father then at her mother. Apparently, their silence meant it was all right for her to answer. She looked back at Katya and nodded.

"I understand that the investigator, Masterkov, has been here to talk with you."

Again, Kurilova just nodded.

"Could you tell me what he wanted to know?"

This time Natalia Kurilova spoke. "Yes, actually he was very kind. He wanted to know if I had ever seen Olga with Mr. Haynes, or whether Olga had ever mentioned Mr. Haynes to me. I said no, I had never seen Mr. Haynes, and that Olga had never said anything about him."

"Did Masterkov say anything about that?"

"No."

"Natalia, when Olga was killed did you think Olga had a relationship with anyone or was seeing anyone?"

Again, Natalia glanced toward her parents. Her mother nodded slightly.

"Well, Olga was a beautiful woman. She had men friends occasionally. I kind of thought she might be seeing someone."

"Why did you think that?" Katya followed up.

"I don't know, just a feeling I guess. I occasionally overheard parts of cell phone conversations she was having. It just seemed like Olga was talking to a man."

"What else did Masterkov want to know?"

"He asked me to tell him more about Olga's investigation that I had mentioned in the statement that I had given him in the patrol car outside Olga's apartment."

"What did you tell him?"

Again, there was a moment of silence, as Natalia looked at her parents. As before, silence apparently meant she could continue. "I said I really didn't know anything more about it than I had already told him. He asked me if it involved the oil and gas companies. I said yes, but that was all I knew. I don't think Investigator Masterkov believed me."

The sound of shattering glass and the eruption of brain matter from Dudinov's head occurred simultaneously. As the three women shrieked in terror, Kurilov yanked his wife and daughter to the floor, pulling them with him to what little protection the cabin wall could provide. Chávez and Katya collided as they too dove downward. On the floor, Chávez pulled himself next to Dudinov's lifeless body and with his right hand felt for Dudinov's nine-milimeter Makarov. However, just as he found it, a shot from Kurilov's rifle exploded, and a body fell through the opening where the window had been a second earlier. Feeling around in the darkness, Chávez located one of Katya's arms and whispered that they needed to crawl to the cabin wall. She made no response, seemly inert and frozen in fear. Forcefully, Chávez grabbed her around the waist with his free arm and pulled her across the floor with him as he made their way to a large beam near the cabin door that Chávez believed would give them the only real protection from the next round of automatic weapon fire.

Just as Chávez had wedged their bodies against the beam he heard footsteps on the cabin porch followed immediately by a fusillade of bullets that ripped through the front door of the cabin. Seconds later a man burst through the shattered front door, his weapon on full automatic. In the dark, the man did not see Chávez now crouched beside the large beam of the doorframe. Chávez had Dudinov's Makarov only inches from the man's head when he blew it apart. It exploded just as another man's head had exploded over thirty years before in the Central Highlands of Vietnam. His vow never to take another life had been broken. As the man fell, Kurilov motioned Chávez toward the shattered window.

Chávez, fighting hard not to vomit and to control his chattering teeth and cramping leg muscles, remained at the window until the sun came up, peering over the dead man's torso that oozed blood from a chest wound and numerous cuts in the stomach area from the remaining shards of glass.

As the sun reached over the horizon, Kurilov told Chávez to stay with the women while he surveyed the perimeter of the cabin and the surrounding trees for other assailants.

For the first time since the bullet sprayed Dudinov's blood and brain matter on each of them, Chávez surveyed the damage to the cabin. The door had been shattered by the high-powered automatic weapon fire. Many of the walls were now pockmarked with embedded slugs. Blood soaked large areas of the cabin's pine floor. Natalia and her mother were squeezed into a corner of the cabin, their arms around each other. Katya was now in what resembled a fetal position, her back still wedged against the cabin wall. She only nodded in response to Chávez's softly intoned inquiries whether she was okay. After surveying the damage, Chávez returned to the window, dragged the body hanging there the remainder of the way through the window, and laid the body next to the other assassin missing most of the back of his head as a result of Chávez's close-range head shot. Although the cold and shock of the event made it hard to control his movements, Chávez searched each of the assassins and Dudinov. Neither of the assassins had any identification. However, the one that Chávez had shot in the back of the head had a cell phone that Chávez put in his right jacket pocket. In his left pocket he placed Dudinov's cell phone and identification.

About a half hour later Kurilov returned to the cabin. "There were at least three of them. I followed tracks back out to the road. There was another car. Dudinov's car appears to be untouched." Kurilov spoke loudly as if making a military combat after action report. Then, turning to Chávez directly, Kurilov exclaimed in a low menacing voice, "How could you do this to us?"

Chávez's first response was to shake his head. Then he managed to speak. "I have no idea who it is that found us. However, it's clear Natalia is in danger. Someone knows about her and wants her—wants all of us—dead. We have to get some protection."

Mr. Kurilov responded, his face expressionless. "No, it's you that needs protection. I can protect my family."

Just as Chávez started to respond, Dudinov's cell phone in the left pocket of Chávez's jacket began to vibrate. He pulled the phone from his pocket, flipped it open, and answered hello in Russian. A young woman's smoke-husky voice asked, "Is this Ivan Dudinov?" Chávez ignored the pending question. Instead he replied, "Is this Tatiana?"

CHAPTER

30

Masterkov had never been inside the gates of the American Village. He assumed, however, that the neatly-groomed lawns surrounding the well-maintained houses and duplexes were intended to mimic a typical American neighborhood. Katya Osipova had reached him on his cell phone about an hour earlier. There was palpable fear in her voice. She said she had to take a chance on him, that she and Chávez needed his help. She would not tell him where she and Chávez were in the American Village. He would need to come to the main gate; things would happen from there.

The American guard at the gate directed Masterkov to a parking spot outside the gate. Masterkov could see Chávez and Osipova silhouetted inside the lighted security building. They both looked extremely tired and edgy. As soon as he entered the security building two American guards patted him down, took everything out of the small leather case he carried, and examined the contents. That included the two-inch MSP pistol, his cell phone, and other personal items. They checked his cell phone thoroughly. However, the guards paid no attention to his key chain. He had activated the recording device located in what appeared to be his car door opener as soon as he entered the security building.

Katya Osipova spoke first. "Investigator Masterkov, thank you for coming. I have told Mr. Chávez that I believe you will help us. I think that deep down you are like me—you believe in the new Russia. Am I right, Alexander Sergeevich?"

Masterkov was not interested in contemplating that question. He wanted to know why he had been called in the middle of the night. What was it about this case that could not wait until morning? But those were simple, mundane thoughts. He had other, more prominent thoughts, ones that had been with him since Professor Sergov told him that even in a country as corrupt and treacherous as Russia it was possible not to succumb to it. He had tried to do that in his own Russian way. He had the sense that in an instant he would have to make a choice that would have the potential to alter his life forever.

"Ms. Osipova, I don't know what you want from me. And I doubt that I am the person you are hoping for. But I am here, and I will listen to what you and Mr. Chávez have to say. So, what is it?"

At that instant, Chávez moved in front of Katya. For the first time since Masterkov had observed Chávez closely, he could see a mask of rage and anger spread across Chávez's face. "Listen, you son of a bitch. I am sick of you and this whole fucking country. You people are the most dysfunctional sons of bitches I have ever seen. This ought to be the most powerful country in the world—

hell, you've got a good share of the world's gas and oil. But you are a bunch of lying, murdering bastards that just destroy each other and everything around you."

Masterkov was just about to turn and leave when Osipova shouted, "Peter, please stop! Alexander Sergeevich, Dudinov is dead. They tried to murder all of us at the Kurilov cabin. There could be a bomb under my car."

Masterkov tried to remain impassive at the shocking assertions. Either someone had settled a score with Dudinov and everyone else was collateral, or his worst fears were now realized. Dudinov and Chávez had bored too deep, and—just maybe—Jonathan Haynes was not Olga's killer. It really did not matter which was the case. By morning the international press would have everything. He could no longer contain things.

"Ms. Osipova, who tried to murder you, and where did this happen?"

Although he directed the question at Katya, Masterkov suspected it would be Chávez that answered, and it would be Chávez who controlled things the rest of the way. He was right.

Again, Chávez raised his voice, sarcasm present in every word. "Investigator Masterkov, I'm going to tell you what happened because, frankly, I don't give a shit what you do. I intend to call reporters from the *International Herald* and others. They will be all over this. You and the rest of the slime you call a Prokuror's Office or a justice system can do whatever the hell you want."

Again, Masterkov wanted to respond, to at least defend himself personally. But that might show emotions that could later cause him trouble. "Mr. Chávez, I am the senior investigator in this region. I now officially request that you respond to my questions. Under Russian law you are required to answer my questions."

"Oh, bullshit. Cut the crap, Masterkov. I said I would tell you what happened," Chávez snapped back.

"So tell me then," Masterkov replied forcefully, keeping his eyes locked on Chávez.

"Dudinov found Natalia Kurilova in Tymovskoye. But you already knew that she was there. Did you tell Karpov where he could find Kurilova?"

Karpov! Why did Chávez immediately mention Karpov? "Is Kurilova still alive?" Masterkov asked in reply.

"I asked you a question. Answer that question first. Did you tell Karpov you had found Kurilova?"

Again, Masterkov knew he had to make a choice. He decided on conciliation. "No, Karpov does not know that I had found Kurilova. She had no information to provide. Why do you want to know?"

"That's my business for now. Kurilova is alive. There were at least three of them who found us at the Kurilov cabin. They first shot Dudinov, but somehow the rest of us survived. Two of them are dead. A third apparently fled."

Masterkov envisioned the bloody mess in the rustic but homey cabin where he had interviewed Natalia Kurilova. He made a mental note that Chávez was careful not to admit that he was responsible for the deaths of either of the assasins. In any event Masterkov had no doubt Mr. Kurilov had protected all of them. "Where are Natalia Kurilova and her family?" Masterkov asked sternly.

"She is safe, that's really all you need to know for now. Let's talk about Karpov, and let's talk about who murdered Sergei Egorov. At first, I thought you might have murdered Egorov. Dudinov told me that he had found the GPS tracking device. He assumed you put it there, and you knew that he had found Egorov. Did you murder that poor bastard? Or did Karpov?"

Karpov again! Why did Chávez constantly refer to Karpov? Now Chávez had accused Karpov of killing Egorov. It was obvious to Masterkov that Kurilova had told Chávez something about Karpov that connected him to Sergova.

"Mr. Chávez, as you know, I am the senior investigator in the region. I don't murder people. I did not murder Egorov or anyone else. Even if I choose to help you, I can't help you if you don't tell me what you think any of this has to do with the case against your client. May I remind you that your client confessed to strangling Sergova?"

Again, Katya Osipova intervened. "Stop it, both of you. Alexander, please, you know what you did with Jonathan Haynes in the interrogation room. Kurilova is safe, and she is willing to testify that Sergova had information that the gas pipeline construction contracts were rigged. Karpov and the Governor rigged them. They probably pocketed millions. You can't deny that journalists are murdered here for investigating a lot less."

Katya continued. "It is very plausible that Sergova's was a contract murder, set in motion by Karpov or the Governor or the contractors. Someone offered Egorov $10,000 to kill Sergova. I think the killer was watching

Sergova and took advantage of her relationship with our client. It was a perfect setup for the killer. He did not have to shoot Sergova. However, it was not Egorov—he had an alibi. Whoever contacted Egorov likely concluded he was too unreliable. You know how he lived. Now Egorov is dead. In any event, you can interview Natalia Kurilova right now. "

Masterkov set his facial muscles. He would not react. However, his mind raced through the investigation. Sergova's unlocked door when Kurilova arrived, her clothes folded by the bed, the missing cell phone and destroyed computer, the prostitute Tatiana who worked for his cousin Nadezhda, the photo of Sergova that he had found in Egorov's tiny apartment just like the prostitute had described. He could already hear Chávez's closing argument to the jury—that is, if any of it got in front of the jury. Chávez and Osipova had no idea about the things he knew about Vasilyuk's private life and the pressure he could put on Vasilyuk if he chose to do so—the Kremlin's influence or not. But that was his business.

"Mr. Chávez, do you really think you can come to this country and publicly accuse our Prokuror General of some kind of crime? You can't really think you will be permitted to do that?"

Masterkov could not believe it, a smile actually appeared on Chávez's face. "Investigator, I am a decent judge of people. Your response tells me you know that events are now out of your control. You can't contain any of this."

Chávez then pulled a cell phone from his pocket and thrust it in Masterkov's direction. "Here is a cell phone that I took from one of the men sent to murder us. If you go to the cabin, he's the one with the back of his head missing. Maybe you can figure out who made the calls received on that phone—that is, if you don't lose the fucking thing. Perhaps you can figure out if there are calls on there that can be connected to Karpov."

Chávez, staring intently, concluded, "If you are not as corrupt as the rest of this godforsaken country, it's time to do the right thing."

Masterkov ignored Chávez's last invective and instead responded, "Please bring Natalia Kurilova here so that I can interview her."

CHAPTER

31

Chávez awoke to unfamiliar surroundings. He was in one of the guesthouses in the American Village, usually reserved for visiting Exxon executives from Houston. Quickly he replayed the remarkable events from the previous evening. He had driven Dudinov's car back from Tymovskoye heading first to Katya's apartment. However, as soon as they had entered Katya's apartment she told him that she felt certain someone had been there. Acting on a hunch, Chávez had told the women to stay in the apartment while he and Mr. Kurilov went to look at Katya's car. With a flashlight Chávez had attempted to determine whether a bomb was attached to the car. His inspection was inconclusive; nevertheless, he had decided that they should not use Katya's car. When he returned to the apartment Katya was already on her cell phone arranging for their lodging at the American Village.

Soon after Masterkov had left the American Village, Chávez and Katya had been directed to one of the larger guesthouses on the property, the Kurilovs to another—their lodging and security arranged from Seattle by John

Hemann, one of Katya's partners in the international law firm. Chávez and Katya had worked together for a while at a large table going over the shocking events at the Kurilov's cabin, planning as best they could a strategy for the courtroom confrontation that would occur in the morning.

They had retired around midnight to separate bedrooms. Chávez had just turned out the light on the bedside table when his door opened and Katya appeared clad in a terrycloth robe. Neither of them said a word as Katya slid under the covers next to him. Although she had said nothing, Peter reached for her and put his arms around her. At first she sobbed quietly, as her body spasmed repeatedly. Eventually, she told Peter that she was frightened beyond anything she ever imagined, even in Russia. Peter was sure that his attempts to assure her that they would get through it were inadequate. As the spasms subsided Katya unwrapped Peter's arms, removed her robe and pressed her naked body tightly to his. Their lovemaking was instantly natural, as if they had been lovers before and had come together again after years of separation, more experienced, more patient, and each more committed to satisfying the other.

Chávez turned his head and looked at Katya. She was lying on her back, her blonde hair framing her beautiful face. He focused first on her full lips that had kissed him so passionately just hours before. As he lay next to Katya's naked body, remembering how his hands had explored the curve of her waist and the perfect lines of her long legs, Katya stirred, opened her eyes, and smiled.

They traveled to the courthouse in two black Land Rovers. Katya and Chávez in the lead vehicle followed by the Kurilovs close behind. Each Land Rover had an armed American driver and guard, former special forces operators employed as security by ExxonMobil.

Natalia Kurilova would testify if Judge Vasilyuk would permit her. Chávez had prepared his argument for Judge Vasilyuk and his questions for Natalia Kurilova. She was nervous but resolute—her father would be at her side every step of the way. Chávez wondered how long it would be before Natalia simply disappeared, choosing the reliable protection of her father.

Masterkov, on the other hand, had left the American Village committing only to interview Natalia Kurilova and to immediately dispatch a bomb detection unit to examine Katya's car and criminalists to the Kurilov cabin. However, Masterkov seemed to convey the message that, for him, little had changed. He had twice reminded Chávez that Jonathan Haynes had lied to him about knowing Sergova. Masterkov also claimed that Dudinov could have orchestrated everything with Egorov and then murdered him. Chávez knew that Masterkov was right. Chávez had no other evidence to corroborate the claim that Karpov was corrupt and that Olga Sergova had discovered it. It remained unclear to Chávez whether Katya's instincts regarding Masterkov were correct. He was just too hard to read.

Tatiana was really Jonathan's only hope. Their conversation on Dudinov's cell phone had been brief. She had returned to Yuzhno. However, when Chávez revealed that Dudinov was dead, she had refused to confirm that

Dudinov's representations were true and had refused to meet or reveal her whereabouts in the city. Chávez had no way to find her. There had been no time to tell Jonathan any of it. He would hear it for the first time in the cage in the courtroom.

Barbatov, exhibiting a confident air, entered the courtroom. From Barbatov's demeanor Chávez surmised that he knew nothing of the events that had transpired in the past twenty-four hours. Barbatov expected a guilty verdict in short order, his 100 percent conviction rate intact.

Judge Vasilyuk entered the courtroom with his usual flourish. Nothing in his facial expression indicted whether he knew anything of the recent events or even cared. "Mr. Chávez, do you have anything further for me to consider before we prepare the verdict form for the jury?"

Chávez was shocked. Did Vasilyuk somehow think Jonathan would not testify in his own defense? Or was that subject to judicial discretion in Russia, like so many of the procedures guaranteeing fairness in American courtrooms and that American lawyers took for granted?

"Your Honor, yes, I do have a matter for the court." Chávez replied, his voice tinged with sarcasm. "Perhaps Your Honor forgot that Mr. Haynes wishes to exercise his right to testify in front of the jury. However, I have another much more serious matter I wish to bring to Your Honor's attention before we bring in the jury."

Although Barbatov immediately sprang to his feet and began to argue, Chávez continued in a loud voice. "Your Honor, Ms. Natalia Kurilova is available, and I would like to put her on the witness stand. My motion to do so is already on file. I do have more to add to my motion, however. Yesterday, three assassins tried to murder Ms. Kurilova, her parents, Ms. Osipova, and me. Our investigator, Ivan Dudinov, was killed. We barely escaped. Likely a bomb was attached to Ms. Osipova's car."

Chávez then paused, listening to the international press in the first row begin to buzz, oblivious to courtroom decorum. For the first time in the trial Judge Vasilyuk banged his gavel and demanded quiet in the courtroom, his face contorted in anger. Chávez turned slightly toward the cage and winked at Jonathan.

In the old days the reporters would have been uncertain what to do. Should they run from the courtroom to call their editor or stay in the courtroom, afraid there was more to come that they might miss? However, this was the twenty-first century. Each reporter started typing on his or her laptop. As Chávez expected, Judge Vasilyuk was outraged.

"Mr. Chávez, Ms. Osipova, Mr. Barbatov, come into my chambers immediately. Do not speak to anyone. Bailiffs keep the press away from the lawyers."

Chávez was still uncertain how much he would reveal. He had no idea what would happen if he accused Karpov in public with so little proof. He might be jailed immediately—hell, they might all be locked up. Vasilyuk was standing behind his desk. Chávez instantly noticed that Judge Vasilyuk's hands were shaking.

"Mr. Chávez, you have stepped over the line with your American courtroom circus-like antics. I have called for the Prokuror General and Investigator Masterkov; unfortunately, my staff can't reach either of them."

Although it was clear that Judge Vasilyuk was just getting started, Chávez interjected.

"Your Honor, I suspect that Investigator Masterkov is in Tymovskoye at the Kurilov cabin sorting through three dead bodies, as I was about to explain in the courtroom."

Judge Vasilyuk held up his hand almost as if to strike Chávez. "Enough, Mr. Chávez. I could imprison you right now." Then Vasilyuk turned to Barbatov. "Mr. Barbatov, where is your boss?"

In a barely audible voice Barbatov replied, "I don't know, perhaps out of town. I did not see him this morning before I came to court."

"Mr. Chávez, I will not permit you to turn this into one of those farcical American trials. You will not speak to the press again, or I guarantee that you will not leave Russia for a long time, if ever. Right now, the fact that this man Dudinov was murdered means nothing. Is there something more?"

Chávez chose his words carefully. "I understand, Your Honor. I believe all of us were targets. Dudinov was working for us as an investigator. He located Natalia Kurilova at her parents' home in the remote village of Tymovskoye. As I have explained before, I believe Ms. Kurilova has information the jury should hear." Then Chávez paused, still uncertain how much to reveal. A middle ground formed in his head. "Ms. Kurilova will testify that she worked closely with Olga Sergova, that Sergova had received information that government influence peddling had occurred in the granting of the oil and natural gas pipeline construction contracts."

Judge Vasilyuk broke in, "So what, do you have any actual evidence that this occurred and that Sergova was targeted?"

Judge Vasilyuk was not dumb. He knew Chávez did not have enough.

"We had a man, Egorov, who said he was approached about a contract to murder Sergova, but as you know he is also dead.. However, Your Honor, the jury should at least hear from Ms. Kurilova about the investigation. As you know, journalists all over Russia have been killed in the last five years. At least fourteen, I believe."

Judge Vasilyuk answered him swiftly. "No, Mr. Chávez. This case will go to the jury tomorrow. I will not allow you to besmirch any officials, even unnamed ones, and to pollute the jury with this rubbish. You should begin preparing your closing argument to the jury."

Chávez was sure his face was unable to hide the scorn that he then felt for Vasilyuk and the whole so-called Russian justice system. "Your Honor, again, perhaps you have forgotten, my client wishes to exercise his right to testify on his own behalf. Surely you don't intend to deny him that right," Chávez stated forcefully.

Judge Vasilyuk smiled. "Of course not. Your client may testify. But that is the last witness this jury will hear."

Chávez had to make one last request, however. "Your Honor, I also filed a request to question Investigator Masterkov in front of the jury. The jury needs to understand the circumstances of my client's statements to Masterkov during the interrogation. It's only fair."

Again, Vasilyuk was swift. "No, Mr. Chávez. You will not be permitted to drag Investigator Masterkov before the jury. I gave you a gift during the pretrial period. It was unprecedented in Russian law. Your questions in the pretrial hearing failed to show me that the statements were not voluntary. Let me repeat: you failed when you had the chance. Mr. Haynes is your last witness. Tomorrow I will send the case to the jury. You utter one more word to the press, and I will jail you and Ms. Osipova immediately. It will be months before you will get any kind of hearing."

CHAPTER

32

Masterkov had no choice but to make the long drive to Tymovskoye. En route, he had been informed by the supervisor of the bomb unit that they had removed a bomb from Katya's car. The bomb had been rigged to explode on ignition. Masterkov's game warden friend had confirmed by cell phone the carnage at the Kurilov cabin. Masterkov had arrived at the cabin only minutes ahead of the forensic team that included Popov.

Dudinov had taken a bullet just above his right eye, blowing out most of the top and right side of his head. The two dead assassins appeared to be Georgians. Unsurprisingly, neither carried any identification. To Popov's complete surprise, Masterkov ordered Popov to use his laptop to check each of the assassins' fingerprints against the fingerprints on Olga Sergova's computer. There was no match.

All the way to Tymovskoye and back to Yuzhno, Masterkov had reviewed the events of the previous evening. Why did Katya Osipova and Chávez think he was different, that he was not completely corrupt like so many of the *militsiya* and government officials in Russia?

Obviously, Osipova did not know that he had searched Chávez's room on numerous occasions, had eavesdropped, and had recorded every one of the meetings she and Chávez had had with Haynes in the Detention Center. Had Dudinov not discovered the tracking device, Masterkov might have prevented the events at Kurilov's cabin. He was a survivor. That was all he could claim so far.

Barbatov had reached him on his cell phone during his return trip to Yuzhno. He described the disclosures that Chávez had made in court and sought Masterkov's confirmation of the events at the Kurilov cabin. Barbatov was ecstatic that Judge Vasilyuk would not permit Chávez to put Natalia Kurilova on the stand in front of the jury. The case would go to the jury the next day. Masterkov had waited for Barbatov's outrage over Chávez's accusations against Karpov, but Barbatov had said nothing about it. When Masterkov inquired about Karpov, Barbatov informed him that Karpov had not been in his office all day and had not answered his cell phone.

As Masterkov entered the outskirts of Yuzhno he checked the Internet on his BlackBerry. The *International Herald* reported that Dudinov had been killed and that there had been an attempt to kill Chávez, Osipova, and the Kurilovs. However, there was nothing about the oil and gas pipeline contracts and the bribing of government officials. Karpov's name was not mentioned. It appeared that Chávez was being cautious.

Masterkov was exhausted by the events of the earlier evening and the grueling drive to Tymovskoye and back. He longed to return to the comfortable confines of his apartment, free for a few hours from the high wire that he had been forced to walk since Olga Sergova's murder. Perhaps with some rest he could chart a course through the tangled mess that now confronted him.

Masterkov's cell phone rang again just seconds after Barbatov had hung up. He quickly glanced at the number on his phone screen. It was Vladimir, one of his trusted operatives in the city who somehow could put any cell phone number together with a name or an identity. Masterkov had given him the cell phone before leaving the city for Tymovskoye.

"Yes, do you have something?" Masterkov answered in a stern voice.

"Take it easy," the voice on the other end replied. "I checked every number, but you only need to know about one."

"OK, give it to me," Masterkov replied.

"Well, okay, you are not going to believe this. One of those cell numbers comes from a SIM card that your friend the Prokuror General purchased. I can tell you where and when he bought the card. And I have confirmed through the cell tower data that he has used the phone from his apartment. I also have the other names for you."

"Okay, that's all I need for now," Masterkov replied calmly, not revealing that his worst suspicion had just been confirmed.

"I will call you in a couple of days, and we can talk about the rest of the names. As usual, this goes nowhere but between us." Masterkov clicked off the phone and headed toward the nicest area of the city.

He drove slowly by Karpov's upscale apartment building. There were no lights visible in the windows of Karpov's fifth-floor apartment. Masterkov slowed, turned down a side street, and pulled behind a row of rickety metal structures that served as car garages for the well-heeled apartment residents. He turned off the engine and sat in the darkened car.

He had never taken a bribe. However, he had done whatever was necessary to navigate through the corrupt and dangerous Soviet law enforcement system. And, for the last fifteen or so years, he had done the same under the so-called new Russian constitutional system of government.

Despite his best efforts, he kept seeing the face of his mentor, Professor Sergov, and hearing his voice—a voice from the past that he could not silence. The investigation and the trial had to be fair. Olga's memory required that it be so.

Someone had killed Dudinov. However, Dudinov might not have been the principal target. It might have been Natalia Kurilova or even Chávez. Really, it did not matter. Something was wrong, however. Where was Karpov? Karpov had monitored every aspect of the case. Now it seemed he could not be contacted. Masterkov got out of the truck and headed toward the apartment building keeping the darkened fifth-floor windows of Karpov's apartment in sight. Unfortunately, Masterkov had no idea where Karpov parked his car or whether Karpov's car was in one of the closed metal sheds. Using an untraceable cell phone Masterkov called Karpov's official cell phone number for the third time since talking to his operative.

And for the third time the call went directly to voice mail. Just before entering the building he called Karpov's residence landline. There was no answer, and no light appeared in Karpov's windows.

Getting into Karpov's apartment would require some work. As was typical with top-floor apartments in most modern Russian apartment buildings, Karpov had installed a heavy metal screen apparatus with a metal door that had to be penetrated in order to reach the outer door to the apartment. If Karpov actually was in the apartment, Masterkov would tell him that he thought it important to inform him about the carnage in Tymovskoye. Masterkov pressed the buzzer that was intended to let the resident know there was someone at the outer door seeking entry. There was no reply. Masterkov buzzed again and waited. Again, there was no response. After waiting another five minutes Masterkov used a small battery-powered lock pick that he had taken from a burglar he had arrested years before to dismantle the lock on the metal door. If Karpov was in the apartment and had ignored the buzzer, he was nevertheless likely to hear the noise of the pick device.

With the small MSP pistol concealed in his right hand, Masterkov banged loudly on the door. No sound came from inside the apartment. The door to the apartment required only a small screwdriver and two small picks. He was inside Karpov's apartment in less than a minute.

Once inside, Masterkov stood perfectly still for a couple of minutes letting his eyes adjust to the darkened apartment. Then, stepping softly, Masterkov checked each room. Clothes remained in the dresser drawers and were hanging in the closet. However, Masterkov could not find a razor, a toothbrush, or any of the items usually found in a man's bathroom. The evidence was inconclusive. Karpov could be on the run or returning in a few minutes, or actually hiding in the apartment. Masterkov had no time to check for every possible hiding place.

In the study Masterkov located a computer. There could be evidence of Karpov's financial activities, and Masterkov had a way to access the computer's hard drive. It was worth a look. He pulled the window shades down and then pressed the computer's On button. From a small bag that he had carried with him into the apartment, Masterkov drew out a six-inch rectangular device that he attached to the computer. In a matter of seconds, the device had by-passed any password or access codes, and Masterkov could roam freely through Karpov's received and sent e-mails. However, just as he did so, the software now running from the device alerted him that six hours earlier someone had run a program designed to erase a number of selected files and e-mails. Quickly, Masterkov brought up an erased file. The file was entitled Ru-Bear Consulting. Soon the entries, one by one, came across the screen.

Ru-Bear Consulting was registered in Khabarovsk ostensibly to provide consulting services regarding the construction of the natural gas and oil pipelines. Copies of invoices now appeared on the screen requesting payment for consulting services rendered to four different pipeline construction companies. The fees sought totaled more than $2 million. Masterkov's mind shot ahead of the computer. Karpov had formed the company in order to permit the construction companies to record bribery payments as legitimate business expenses.

Quickly he downloaded the remaining contents of the file and the erased e-mails. Ru-Bear Consulting did business with a bank in Macau, the island turned over to China by Portugal in 1999 when the British left Hong Kong. Since then it had become a well-known financial center.

Masterkov somehow sensed the movement of air behind him. Instinctively, he thrust his left forearm up and backward, deflecting the hand wielding a large knife from its path toward the middle of Masterkov's back. Instead, the knife sliced only air. Although Masterkov had managed to deflect the path of the knife, the attacker entangled Masterkov in a bear hug pulling them both to the floor. Masterkov was on the bottom staring directly into Karpov's expressionless face. Somehow Masterkov managed to grip Karpov's left wrist with his right hand trying to force the knife from Karpov's hand. Karpov's right hand was locked on Masterkov's left wrist. The small MSP pistol was now inaccessible— he had placed it back in the small holster and in the tumble the holster and pistol had slid too far around his right hip and was now causing severe pain in his back. Masterkov realized that he had only seconds to hold off the knife that Karpov was trying with all is strength to force into Masterkov's neck. Karpov was just too strong to overpower. There was, however, one opening. Masterkov's left leg was free. In an instant and in one quick motion Masterkov drew his knee up and rammed it with all of his strength into Karpov's testicles. Karpov recoiled and screamed in pain. It was just enough to permit Masterkov to reverse their positions. Forcing all his weight downward, both hands grasping Karpov's left hand and wrist, Masterkov drove the knife into the left side of Karpov's chest, burying the knife up to its hilt. Masterkov was unsure if the blade had penetrated Karpov's lung or heart, but he knew it had hit one of them and was so deep that Karpov would be gone in seconds.

"Did you order a hit on Olga Sergova, you son of a bitch?" Masterkov shouted.

Blood bubbled from Karpov's mouth muffling and distorting the sounds that appeared to be uttered in reply. In seconds the sound stopped, and Masterkov thought he could see the life leave Karpov's eyes. Karpov was dead.

Masterkov slowly raised himself from the corpse and leaned against the computer desk. His body went limp, and Masterkov assumed he was going into some kind of shock. During his career he had been involved in a number of physical encounters; however, he had always had the advantage, and he had never killed another human being. Now, in just seconds, he had killed the island's Prokuror General with a knife. Of course, had he not fought back Karpov would have killed him. Karpov somehow knew Masterkov was headed in his direction or somehow saw him heading into the apartment building. He had no time to figure out how that was so. Apparently, Karpov chose the knife over a gun because he was worried about the sound of gunshot and inability to control blood spatter from a gunshot wound.

As Masterkov calmed himself and concentrated on normalizing his breathing, he looked around the apartment. The scene was not complicated. Had he been able to reach his pistol he would have had to dig a slug out of the body or even a wall to avoid the possibility that the slug could be linked to his pistol. The knife was not a problem because it apparently came from Karpov's kitchen. Other than the immediate area where he and Karpov had struggled nothing else was disturbed. Still, Masterkov had to make a decision, and he had to make it at that instant—call another investigator to the scene and explain the whole thing or simply walk away. He chose the latter.

Quickly, Masterkov made a mental inventory of everything he might have touched. Donning a pair of rubber gloves Masterkov yanked the knife out of Karpov's chest, and used his handkerchief to wipe down the knife. He wrapped the knife in his handkerchief and placed the items in his coat pocket for future disposal. Masterkov then grabbed a kitchen towel and wiped down every surface that he could have touched. His training and experience told him that he had likely lost hair and skin tissue and other trace evidence that, under the right circumstances, could be used to identify him. Carefully, Masterkov scraped the inside of each of Karpov's fingernails hoping to remove any of his own skin fragments containing his DNA that might have gotten under Karpov's nails during the struggle. There was, however, no time to vacuum the floor and the body. In any event, Masterkov would later orchestrate the official entry into the apartment and his presence at that time should account for any trace evidence placing him in Karpov's apartment.

Although Masterkov was confident that he had left the apartment undetected, he knew that his career and his life in Russia were in great jeopardy. Every muscle in his body ached, and his hands still trembled a bit. However, he could not yet return to his apartment. He had four things he had to do before the court proceedings began at nine the next morning. The results of the first three things would dictate whether he undertook the fourth.

CHAPTER

33

Chávez stood in front of the bathroom sink and stared at himself in the mirror. He still had no real evidence with which to save Jonathan Haynes. He could not think of a single trial in which he'd had less to work with, at least any trial that he had won. Without some intervention before the closing argument, Jonathan Haynes would likely die in a Russian prison, either violently or of some disease. As Chávez suspected, and despite his protests, Natalia Kurilova and her parents disappeared as soon as Judge Vasilyuk said he would not permit Natalia to testify. When court had ended for the day, Chávez, over Katya's strong protest that it was too dangerous, had gone to the Eurasia Hotel searching for Tatiana. The search was quick and unsuccessful. A six-foot-seven bouncer with a shaved head, wearing a full-length black leather coat and a large Glock visible under his coat, unceremoniously escorted Chávez from the hotel bar. With every ounce of will he could muster, Chávez parked each negative thought in a corner of his brain. He had no idea how the day would end. If things went horribly wrong he could end up sitting in a jail cell next to his client. There was, however, one thing in Russia that was very right in his life.

Just as Chávez touched the razor to his lathered face, Katya walked into the small bathroom, turned on the shower, and stepped in. As the beginning waves of steam drifted from the shower, the glass door opened and a hand reached out and beckoned him to enter.

* * * * * * * * * *

Barbatov was already in the courtroom when Chávez and Katya entered. Barbatov's hair, freshly oiled, glistened as he arranged the contents of the investigative file that he would likely refer to during his closing argument.

Jonathan was in the cage. He hardly raised his head when Chávez was permitted to approach the cage. Chávez had no more words of comfort. Instead, he held Jonathan's hand firmly for a few seconds and then turned away, knowing that that could be the last sympathetic touch Jonathan Haynes might ever experience.

As Chávez turned from the cage, Katya's cell phone began to chime. As soon as Katya put the cell phone to her ear, Chávez watched her face change from a look of surprise to concern and then to true excitement. All Chávez could hear of the conversation was Katya repeating, "I understand, I understand."

With her free hand Katya grabbed the shoulder of Chávez's suit, pulling him with her toward the large courtroom doors. As they burst into the hallway, Chávez saw an attractive young blonde woman seated on the hallway bench. At the instant they entered the hallway, Katya exclaimed, "Peter, this woman is Tatiana from the Eurasia Hotel."

Chávez knew that there was no time to waste and rapidly began asking Tatiana Primakova to confirm everything she had told the madam at the hotel. However, before Chávez could complete the conversation, a bailiff demanded that he and Katya return to the courtroom. Judge Vasilyuk was about to take the bench.

As Judge Vasilyuk entered, he stated, "Mr. Barbatov and Mr. Chávez, you will each have one hour to present your closing argument to the jury."

In as strong a voice as he could muster without shouting, Chávez said, "Your Honor, please, before you bring in the jury, I have a matter of grave importance. Your Honor, we have a witness, Ms. Tatiana Primakova. She is here in the courtroom this morning. She can testify that she worked at the Eurasia Hotel. And that on the evening that Olga Sergova was murdered, she was with a customer who had with him a photo of Ms. Sergova and an apartment address written on the back of the photo. Ms. Primakova has just returned from Thailand and is willing to testify this morning."

Barbatov was on his feet instantly, yelling, "Your Honor, this is ridiculous. I am ready to begin my argument to the jury just as you ordered yesterday. It is just another American trick, trying to divert us from the truth of this horrible murder."

To Chávez's amazement, Judge Vasilyuk's face did not exhibit shock or surprise or any of the usual irritation that accompanied Chávez's requests to make the trial truly adversarial. It was as if he expected it.

Vasilyuk ignored Barbatov's shriek and asked Chávez to continue.

"As I explained to you yesterday in your chambers, our investigator, Mr. Dudinov, was murdered two days ago by unknown assailants. As you already know, Mr. Dudinov had previously discovered a man who was approached about the contract murder of Ms. Sergova and that man, Egorov, was killed. I am sure you read in the paper about the discovery of his body. Your Honor, fourteen journalists throughout Russia have been the victims of contract murders over the past few years. Ms. Sergova was investigating corruption of government officials in the awarding of the gas and oil pipeline construction contracts at the time she was killed. Your Honor, our jury must hear this witness in order for Mr. Haynes to have a fair trial. Only then can the world see that Russia's new system truly operates fairly for everyone."

Barbatov screamed again. "We know nothing of this witness. I am sure she is a fake. Besides, it's against our law. A witness may only speak to an investigator. Investigator Masterkov has never interviewed this woman. There must be a report from the investigator. Your Honor, we must begin the closing arguments."

Without acknowledging Barbatov's pleas, Judge Vasilyuk looked toward the rear of the courtroom. Everyone turned. Masterkov was standing near the door.

"Investigator Masterkov, please come forward," Judge Vasilyuk commanded.

As Masterkov walked toward the front of the courtroom, Judge Vasilyuk asked, "Do you have any knowledge of this witness? Have you interviewed her?"

Masterkov answered immediately in a clear, authoritative voice. "Yes, Your Honor, I learned about this witness' presence early this morning. I interviewed her at that time. Prokuror General Karpov is not in his office this morning, so I am now providing a copy of the report of my interview to Mr. Barbatov. I have also done a second interview with Natalia Kurilova. I am also providing a copy of that report to Mr. Barbatov."

Reluctantly, as if the reports were infected with a communicable disease, Barbatov took them from Masterkov's outstretched hand.

"Do you have any more questions for me?" Masterkov asked abruptly, never making eye contact with Chávez or Katya.

For just an instant Chávez thought he saw something in a look that passed between Judge Vasilyuk and Masterkov. Then Vasilyuk said, "No, I require nothing more from you."

Masterkov then returned to a bench in the back of the courtroom.

Judge Vasilyuk turned back to Barbatov. "Mr. Barbatov, I assume you want me to place a copy of the investigator's report in the investigative file that I have in front of me. All of the reports must go to the jury."

Barbatov glanced up from the report. "This is unconscionable. I need time to prepare to question this witness. I need time to investigate her background. She is a prostitute, Your Honor."

Chávez started to respond, "Your Honor," but Vasilyuk held up his hand and said, "Not now, Mr. Chávez."

"Mr. Barbatov, as you have said many times in this courtroom—we seek the truth. Her testimony will not be long or complicated. I am sure, Mr. Barbatov, that a man of your skill in the courtroom will have no trouble questioning this witness. The jury will decide what weight to give Ms. Primakova's testimony and the report of Investigator Masterkov's interview with Ms. Kurilova, which will be provided to the jury with the other investigative file reports."

Barbatov shot back, "We need a recess then. I need to confer with the Prokuror General. You can't do this."

To Chávez's utter and complete amazement, Judge Vasilyuk responded, "No, there will be no recess. It seems that your boss can't be located. The witness will testify now, then Mr. Haynes, then you both will make your closing arguments. Bailiff, bring in the jury."

CHAPTER

34

Masterkov stood in the same out-of-the-way corner of the small international terminal of the Sakhalin airport where he had first observed Chávez's arrival. This time he watched as Chávez and Jonathan Haynes emerged from a throng of reporters headed for the concourse leading to their plane bound for Seoul.

It had only been a few hours since the jury's swift verdict. The jury had unanimously answered no to the second question, "Did the defendant commit the act?" Masterkov had used his small digital recorder to capture Chávez's closing argument. He wanted it for posterity. Chávez had used no notes. He seemed to speak from the heart as he chopped away at Barbatov's claims about the government's proof. He pointed out the inconsistencies in the evidence, Sergova's missing cell phone, the lost nightshirt and panties, and the other missteps that he described as investigative failures. Chávez explained why the panties and nightshirt were important. According to Chávez, what likely happened was that Olga had removed her clothes and folded them neatly near the bed where her Levis and bra had been found. She and

Jonathan then made love. Afterward she put on her night-shirt and her panties. The real killer, who had been watching the apartment, entered Olga's apartment some-time soon after Haynes had left. The locks on her door were easily manipulated. The killer had literally ripped the nightshirt and panties from Olga's body in the strug-gle that ensued. Chávez read from Kurilova's second statement, explaining Olga's investigation. Chávez even read from the copy of the letter Olga had received accus-ing the Governor and Karpov of receiving bribes for their approvals of the successful bidders on the pipeline con-tracts.

Repeatedly, Chávez referred to the powerful testi-mony of Tatiana Primakova and her encounter with the Georgian at the Eurasia Hotel. Barbatov had been unable to shake her in his cross-examination. She had her date-book with her in court, containing an entry showing a customer about ten p.m. on the night of December 20th. Primakova was positive the photo that fell out of the Georgian's coat pocket was of Olga Sergova. Chávez claimed Haynes lied about knowing Sergova because he was frightened and believed the police were corrupt—a powerful argument to the average Russian.

In a soft but firm voice, Chávez explained the mean-ing of the presumption of innocence and proof beyond a reasonable doubt. When Chávez had concluded his argu-ment, Masterkov thought that most of the jurors were ready to let Jonathan Haynes return to America. Never-theless, he still thought a guilty verdict was possible when he saw that the jury had selected the law professor and former prosecutor as its foreperson.

What had Chávez known about the woman juror that Masterkov had missed in his investigation of the potential jurors? The woman had glanced directly at Masterkov as she pronounced in a firm voice, "We answer the second question on the verdict form, 'No.'"

At that instant, Masterkov watched Chávez write in a binder on the counsel table in front of him. Masterkov could barely make out the words, but he thought Chávez had written "Not Guilty, 3:30 in the afternoon, March 14, 2006, Yuzhno-Sakhalinsk, Russia."

Some night, with a good bottle of cognac, Masterkov would review the notes that he had made when Chávez had questioned the law professor and former prosecutor during jury selection. Someday, when no one cared anymore, he just might contact her to learn firsthand why, as foreperson of the jury, she actually facilitated the implementation of the democratic reforms she had indicated to Masterkov's operatives that she opposed.

Masterkov determined that the same software he had encountered at Karpov's apartment computer had been used to erase files from Karpov's office computer. Those deleted files, however, had nothing to do with the pipeline construction contracts. Most of the files concerned other government officials. There was even a file entitled, "Alexander Sergeevich Masterkov." The contents of that file made it clear that Karpov considered Masterkov untrustworthy, an enemy of sorts. The next morning when no one could reach Karpov, Masterkov would suggest that he and another investigator go to Karpov's apartment to check for him.

Masterkov returned to the present as he watched Chávez and Katya Osipova embrace at the door to the concourse. He doubted Osipova would remain on Sakhalin Island for long. Then Chávez turned from her and scanned the small terminal. Eventually, his eyes came to rest on Masterkov. Ever so slightly Chávez nodded in his direction. Chávez knew that Masterkov had located Tatiana Primakova and assured her of her safety, making her testimony possible. Chávez did not know, however, and neither he, nor anyone else, would ever know about Masterkov's early morning visit with Judge Vasilyuk. There were things that only Masterkov knew about Judge Vasilyuk, and Masterkov was certain that his conversation with the judge would remain private forever. Vasilyuk was now in a double bind and his future as a judge surely was in doubt. But that was his problem. As his eyes met Chávez's, Masterkov returned a slight nod, then turned and walked out of the terminal.

Masterkov's instincts and the jury verdict now told him that he had not solved the Olga Sergova murder case. Yet, in light of everything that had transpired, he doubted that Professor Sergov would believe that he had failed him or his daughter. To the extent possible in Russia, the trial had been fair.

An inch of snow had fallen since Masterkov had entered the terminal. It covered the dirty streets and the forlorn buildings of Yuzhno. Everything appeared clean and new. A slight grimace crossed Masterkov's face. Many things in Russia were not as they appeared to be. In the end, there remained the question, would Russia ever free itself from its past?

Epilogue

Judge Peter Chávez stood at the security gate on D concourse of the Portland International Airport. He had a dozen roses with him, prepared to welcome Katya to the City of Roses.

Nearly a year had elapsed since he and Jonathan Haynes had left Russia hours after the verdict. Two days after the verdict, Masterkov announced the discovery of Karpov's body in Karpov's apartment and the subsequent discovery of computer files linking Karpov to bid-rigging in connection with the pipeline projects. Masterkov was leading the investigation of Karpov's murder, which remained unsolved. Similarly, the investigation into the murder of Olga Sergova continued and was unsolved—just like all of the other investigations of the contract murders of journalists throughout Russia.

The Senate Judiciary Committee hearing had little to do with his qualifications and instead centered on the Haynes case and Chávez's firsthand knowledge of the Russian criminal justice system. The confirmation vote was unanimous.

Jonathan Haynes had kept in touch for a few months, but Chávez had not heard from him recently. The Haynes Resources and Development properties were being sold. Jonathan Haynes would never have to work again if he did not want to.

Chávez had a new habit since returning from Russia and starting his career on the federal bench in Portland. Each day, after his morning run, Chávez would read the online English version of *The Moscow Times*. To his dismay the democratic principles expressed in the Russian constitution continued to recede from Russian life. The Kremlin now controlled the television, radio, and print media. Dissent was quickly and brutally suppressed. Russian judges were forbidden from attending any legal education conference underwritten with foreign funds. The mutual cooperation agreement between Russian and American lawyers had never been finalized.

Journalists that investigated governmental corruption or the effect of the Russian mafia on the economic development of the country or Russia's difficult war in Chechnya continued to be murdered. Only days before, Anna Politskovskaya, who had written so eloquently about the Russian abuses in Chechnya, had been gunned down as she stepped off the elevator in her Moscow apartment building. A "control shot" had been administered.

The six weeks that he had spent in the Russian Far East defending Jonathan Haynes had profoundly affected him. Never again would he take America's cumbersome legal system for granted. Each day he appreciated the genius of the founding fathers and the enduring power of the American Constitution to protect the rights of individual Americans.

Despite the torment, the self-doubt, and the outright fear that he had experienced in Russia, there was something about the place and its people that had wedged itself into his psyche. Despite the danger, despite the corruption, there were good people like Katya and even Masterkov who wanted to shake the past. Yet, so many of their countrymen remained prisoners of that past and seemed doomed to repeat it.

Katya came into view. She was stunning, even after the lengthy flights from Sakhalin to Seoul, and then to Seattle and Portland. The empty feelings that had plagued him in the years following Claire's death had lessened. Involuntarily, Chávez rubbed the scar tissue on his left wrist. There was no pain, only the vision of a strong black man who had carried him to safety more than thirty years before. The debt was paid.

THE END

About the Author

Paul J. De Muniz is a Vietnam war veteran and former Oregon appellate judge who served for more than twenty-two years on the bench, including as chief justice of the Oregon Supreme Court. He retired from the Oregon Supreme Court at the end of 2012. De Muniz graduated from Portland State University in 1972 and Willamette University College of Law in 1975. In 2002, De Muniz founded a rule-of-law partnership with judicial leaders in the Russian Far East, working with lawyers and judges in Russia to implement reforms within the Russian criminal justice system. De Muniz is also the author of *A Practical Guide to Oregon Criminal Procedure and Practice* and co-author of *American Judicial Power: The State Court Perspective*, a legal treatise emphasizing the importance of America's state courts. De Muniz currently teaches at Willamette University College of Law as a Distinguished Jurist in Residence.

CPSIA information can be obtained
at www.ICGtesting.com
Printed in the USA
LVOW11s2004180117
521425LV00001B/6/P